We

a reimagined family history

c.vance

art by Debra Di Blasi

We

a reimagined family history
c.vance

art by Debra Di Blasi

Jaded Ibis Press
sustainable literature by digital means.™
an imprint of Jaded Ibis Productions
Seattle, Washington USA

© 2011 copyright c.vance

First edition. All rights reserved.

ISBN: 978–0–9831956–2–7

Library of Congress Control Number: 2011937991

Printed in the United States of America. No part of this book may be used or reproduced in any manner whatsoever without written permission from the publisher, except in the case of brief quotations embodied in critical articles and reviews. For information please email: questions@jadedibisproductions.com

Published by Jaded Ibis Press, *sustainable literature by digital means*™ An imprint of Jaded Ibis Productions, LLC, Seattle, Washington USA http://jadedibisproductions.com

Cover design and interior art by Debra Di Blasi

This book is also available in digital and fine art limited editions. Visit our website for more information.

Editor's Note

We: A Reimagined Family History contains a reading code on the side of each page that deepens the narrative between sections. For example, the code 3.10 indicates the section is told from the point of view of "they" and relates to the theme of "milled lives." If you're so inclined, use this key to decode:

<table>
<tr><td>

First Number
point of view

1 – father
2 – mother
3 – they
4 – we
5 – she

</td><td>

Second Number
theme

1 – set a tone
2 – faulty homages
3 – the world cannot keep standing...
4 – escape
5 – home made
6 – games
7 – where we're from
8 – a beautiful aside
9 – impotent magics
10 – milled lives
11 – growth
12 – Death in the family
13 – what was survived
14 – attractive distractions
15 – war
16 – the end of the world
17 – what was promised
18 – patient resignation
19 – Rebecca
20 – a new end

</td></tr>
</table>

c.vance

we

the world changed when we entered it...

instantly...

maybe not instantly...

maybe things changed a bit before: mother's labor screams warning of unwanted arrivals.

if it wasn't instantly then it was soon after. we were the births that broke this ground. mother told about it each birthday, how we heralded the demise of everything everyone loved. hardly something for which we could be held responsible, but parents inherently shirk the burden of blame— ready to sacrifice offspring if offered another chance at youth; the only reason we were born anyway— when the world no longer is the one they remember.

when rivers began flowing downstream— oceans too tired to continue pushing themselves inland let everything come to them —father was ready to play the part of Abraham in a:

– *Wow. Did you see that coming?*
unBiblical finish until mother stepped in to stop him.

and when mother finally realized the world's changes were insufferable, father's help was requested in obtaining a second-year abortion— but father no longer cared; we were already here and should be made to share in the suffering we brought.

we inherited a world awkwardly anew.

we broke a world impossible to rebuild.

(29,351)

we

father   1.

we

11

c.vance

2.

mother

Father's parents meet in a time of war.

These things set the tone for the rest of people's lives.

Both sixteen as father's father carries father's mother away with a gold ring to impregnate in a tiny apartment's confines before boarding a boat, leaving wife, zygote and ring behind to see what everyone was dying about in the four-year war of '54.

It happens, sometimes, that Time forgets how to measure people who sail seas away. Some return their parents' elder, some never return at all... aged to dust in the time it takes those at home to fall asleep.

So it is with father's parents.

Father's father returns to a bedroom mirror revealing nothing remembered: a heavier body, squinting eyes etched with a decade's documentation of death witnessed. And behind this stranger's reflection sits father's mother, a cigarette in the hand of a seventeen-year-old body fallen to the stillbirthed daughter it nurtured and relinquished eight days before.

These things set the tone for the rest of people's lives.

1.1

Mother's parents say little.

Both capable of getting by on looks alone.

Both believing thoughts do best when they remain only that: thoughts. Which says more, really, than most slick talkers. These young lives determined by seven words, saying them simultaneously while randomly passing paths on a southwestern sidewalk too hot to stop for long.

"Would you like to go with me?"

That is it.

All smiles, mother's father breaks stride toward wherever and turns to walk with mother's mother wherever the destination would be. It works for them. Going to the theater or dinner, one simply goes and the other is there at the hip.

Even their marriage is a happenstance of thought. Mother's mother walks to the altar with measured steps and mother's father follows. A four-year courtship concludes with, "I do."

Nine monosyllabic words used well; these things set the tone for people's lives.

Sometimes it is an honorary title: father.

Like living rooms labeled in abandoned homes.

The boon of lineage deciphers details in an offspring's face to see if the assumption is plausible. But father came third. An older brother held onto this world better than the sibling before them both. So now the disparity between the two inspire constant comparisons, concluding one or the both of them have no ties to the parent who tied a name behind theirs; a lead-ballooned promise on a string constructed to be the mediator that keeps the heavens grounded.

Maybe this is what made father's father mad. Short-tempered, surely, but armed with a laugh instigated by little. A dementia-laugh forcing others to laugh if, for no other reason, than to laugh at the laughter.

Laughter letting father know life could be lived under an assumed name.

1.2

Mother's father builds custom bridges.

It keeps the scenery of mother's childhood shifting. A new town with a hundred new demands: an old lady wanting one built to the tree outside her window to see the world the way of her stuck cat; a young man wanting one constructed to connect him to dreams; a late-twenties lady mailing blueprints of a bridge built from bent moonlight and fog so she could silently escape the life she does not remember choosing; a dozen men wanting a way back to the woman they once loved; a dozen women wanting a way back into the bodies they once had.

Mother's father rarely works a fortnight's worth of work before something moves them again.

It's something in the clientele.

Bridges attract arsonists or, if not something so blatant, careless people with matches. And these acts attract people to mother's father: accusatory lawmen claiming accessory to arson and/or insurance fraud; lynch mobs with constantly dropped torches igniting everything beautiful in their wake; legal jargon slipped beneath the door insisting the structure be rebuilt because it did not live up to the fire codes of the area; delivery boys delivering baskets of bran muffins laced with laxatives or cyanide.

The world cannot keep standing the wondrous things mother's father builds.

Train tracks travel the center of father's family home.

Growing up on both sides as the family of four weekend-watch the television between brumdum drumbum wheels rolling over rivets; hours of entertainment interrupted in the strobed staccato amidst a constant bass rhythm.

Weekdays it babysits father and father's brother. Both parents work nights and sleep away low-volume days in this house where little can ignite unfavorable temperaments. Both boys occasionally looking up to pump fistfuls of prayers for whistles to acknowledge this indiscretion. If it is not given, hands open to wave at teens riding rails away: the only way for teens to escape this town of minds no wider than its one-lane roads to nowhere.

This town where the gynecologist moonlights as a tattoo artist, embroidering ink warnings, "Abandon hope all ye entering the light," at the far end of the birth canal in a language only infants can read. No one tolerates being told anything for their own good.

They now escape into tunneling darkness in search of the contentment no longer known. An exodus of the town's young watch father's confused face ignite white in the monochromatic flicker of the television, then stutter-step back into the shadow of wheels only to ignite white again, as they try to regain hope in becoming destinationless.

1.4

Everything here is a sun-bleached pale.

Not only cracked white houses with matching shingles but also off-white streets and lawns spraypainted to colorlessness. Even the clouds seem in on it, never parting for an exposed blue. An island city where limits contain nothing less monochromatic than a silver screen picture. Nowhere is there even the sepia of old photographs leaking into the landscape. So stagnant that only sly shadows can sometimes sneak forbidden cold colors of periwinkle whims within the river contained borders of a place honest enough not to display, "Welcome!" signs.

Mother's family's heads hold the only flare of brunette hair on the limestone sidewalks of talc-faced onlookers reenacting their favorite silent film lines, all tolerating the impure bronze-skinned troupe for its promise of an iconic covered bridge for the town's entrance. A bridge promising no shadow will hang in its interior.

Other builders tried: one with translucent walls, another over-saturated the wooden cage with 80-watt light. None were capable of completely obliterating the darkness that allows the illusion of color.

Here, mother speaks her first words and recites the alphabet without seeing a letter or a coloring book that is not white-on-white where only the crayon's gloss reveals mother's early tendency to remain within imaginary boundaries.

Two years waiting for sunlight-injected acorns to bring up an orchard of luminescent oak trees large enough to build a covered bridge.

Mother sits in the idling station wagon on the colored side of the river as the last glass nail is driven into the perfect construct radiating white. Tires squeal goodbyes before any praise can be given. Mother's father knows the bridge will be the first thing to burn when tempers ignite over the world to which they are now attached.

4.37

This is where father first feels like a man.

Family following father's mother's cigarette smoke, flower in hand, up to cemetery hill. Father's Sunday suit armpit stained in summer heat, something only seen on the suits of men.

Through just-in-case cast-iron gates and tsch-tsch sprinklers trickle stopping as all approach, the family passes over the newly dead with stone plaques barely visible and walk around the long-dead granite grown into raised headstones. Sprinklers start again behind and die anew in front in respect for the living.

Eventually they stumble upon father's sister's petite stone as sprinklers spring up to water everywhere but where they stand as father's mother wails wails of, "I can't believe she left us, Daddy." Father's father, a hand on the crying woman's shoulder, silently offers thankful prayers to the soul of the only child thoughtful enough not to be a burden.

Father and father's brother sneak away to play hide-and-seek. A game played for second place since the oldest already found the perfect hiding spot. So the last in line invents numbers to fill the gaps between the four known (1, 2, 3 and 20) and the words, "Ready or not, here I come!" Sludging shoes schlep across watered grass as all sprinklers stall in anticipation of father's movements.

The only found man is dark, wearing denim pants and a buttoned flannel on the outskirts among emerald markers contrasting granite. Ready to cheatingly ask about father's brother, but would-be words are interrupted with, "They don't like it."

"Who?"

"The dead. Would you like your home flooded?"

The question is given thought, pros and cons of living underwater weighed: swimming everywhere, fish for friends and never having to worry about finding a toilet. But it is not the right answer, and father is a five-minute-old man of expectations so answers, "No."

The dark man nods and tells how buried pipes flowered into sprinklers controlled by overturning these emerald markers to twist the bones of dead metal tubes. Father listens to these botanical wonders which will influence someday choices. Listens long after father's family leaves and nightfall forces the dark man to escort the young newly man out.

The streetlamp-lit streets home are sprinted down, taking flight from fears of the dead Olly Olly Oxen Free abandoning flooded homes they somehow hate.

Mother is the attractive creation of beautiful people.

Built in the compromised combination of both parents' features, the cursed anti-gestalt of mother and mother's siblings. None living up to the original stone sculpted from… afterthought sketches conjured after the masterpieces were completed.

But physicality is only half of it.

Where siblings understand the statements of the mirror, mother is a three-year-old student of the behavior of the beautiful: smiles promising more than can ever be delivered; eyes that can make a man bold or cower; a walk that punishes all that watch with its memorableness looped and looped and looped in closed eyes seeking sleep that will not come.

Early on, mother learns the finer points of beauty so she will never need to be beautiful.

The fourth year February.

Father and father's father find an eighty-eight-degree Saturday. Snow slushes to transparency on sidewalks unseen in four months. And this man that incessantly complains about the bothersomeness of wife and boys today seeks out father to play outside. There they throw contorted balls of ice around the barren apple tree, hiding behind the few strands of red leaves on the cherry tree. All acts committed in shorts and t-shirts, dashing about the front yard.

Teases of Spring spring bad ideas.

Father's father fires up the old Chevy to the melody of a country song on the radio. Father is grabbed and is placed on father's father's lap to steer down roads of ruts and rivets in the waning melt.

They learn little is more fun than an uncontrollable rear-wheel-drive pickup losing control. So they scream through giggles while wiping out mailboxes, hedges, clotheslines, yard ornaments of marmots and gnomes and toppling a telephone pole at the onset of dark and freezing streets.

In giddy glee they abandon the truck as though no one would know who did it. Their smiles lighting up a newly darkened neighborhood.

Mother's father researches codes in each new city's library.

Mother's sister is in the first year of grade school, mother's brother isn't yet born, and mother's mother refuses to subject skin to the torrents of midday heat.

So today, like most days, mother follows mother's father. Running to the bay of library windows with a scream and wide eyes. Forehead and hands pressing against glass to watch trees sway and brick buildings move against stagnant cloud backdrops until over-excited breathing fogs the view.

Then a meter sprint to the middle of the second window, hands and forehead again against another window. Staying that way, watching brick buildings sway and trees move against stagnant cloud backdrops until it, too, fogs.

Then a meter sprint to the last window, her hands and forehead again against another window. Staying that way and watching swaying trees and red brick buildings move against stagnant cloud backdrops until it, too, fogs.

Mother squeals and giggles and runs back to the first window which clears in anticipation.

And mother's father approaches, open book in hand, telling it is time to go. A command unheard. Grabbing the calloused hand, pulling it the first window to say, "Look!"

And a cursory glance is given at the empty side street and a smile saying in mother's father's silent language, "Yes, honey, that's nice," while walking away.

But mother's small hand is hard to hold long, pulling itself free to run to the second window holding swaying branches and moving brick buildings against stagnant cloud landscapes, saying, "Now look at this one, daddy!"

And, without looking, says aloud, "They're all the same, sweetie."

Mother stares at mother's father as the book takes attention away, watching page after page being read while wondering what other things go unseen.

So mother returns to the windows, back and forth between the three with forehead and hands in place and watches the empty side street one last time. Mother's father looks up from the book and says mother's name.

Mother stops and takes the available callous hand, squeezing it with affection as they leave the library together.

There is a makeshift koi pond in the backyard.

Rocks stacked at one end where the hose is wedged atop to give the water depth as it falls into the garbage bag-lined hole in the ground. It holds six goldfish: the white one named Goldie; the gold one named Scottie and the other white and gold splotched amalgamations of the first two all named Coy. There are no koi.

No one knows the difference.

Not even the goldfish.

Winter came without worry. All sat on the bottom and convinced the water they were like it, freezing when it froze. But summer is here now and the goldfish evaporate in pleas of, "But we're fish!"

True koi never would have let this happen.

1.8

Mother's mother is a full-time student of herself.

Studying the way hand skin gives its tautness away to veins beneath, how elbows become coarse overnight, and staring at stretch-marks like a child with a scab.

Bedtime stories are told by mother's mother about her one focal point, the only thing to motivate words from a silent woman.

"Once upon a time there was a beautiful woman who met a beautiful man and they believed they'd live happily ever after. But the selfish man wanted children. So the beautiful woman gave him children and each of them tore away pieces of her beauty as they were born. None happy to have the life she gave them, they each had to take the one thing the woman possessed. Then only the man was beautiful and no one knew how long he would stick around and watch the woman age."

Crying by the time "The end" is said.

Mother's mother spends unemployed days sitting stone-faced, knowing smiles ruin everything. Sitting until ready to burst with boredom, mother faces mother's mother to contort an eye, twist the tongue and squiggle the left nostril while flaring the right. A face of complete humor.

And mother's mother loses it, explodes into laughter for a brief second, then frowns for the rest of the day at a beauty regiment failed.

Mother does it for the frowns, not the laughter. Already the corners of mother's mother's mouth have etched faint lines into downward trends. In a house of such competition, mother knows she would never naturally win the mantle of most beautiful so the competition is slowly sabotaged.

Neighborhood boys play Kings and Fools.

Jesters of all ages drawing straws to see who will play and which will watch. Father believes it is fixed, always drawing the shortest one. Forced by fortune to regally sit with stick scepter and cardboard crown while every other boy is afforded the luxury of any foolish deed: somersaults, juggling, fire breathing, licking nine volt batteries.

Eventually it concludes with the inevitable sampling of stolen wine from someone's mother's pantry mixed with some toxic concoction pulled from beneath kitchen sinks. One by one acting out their elaborate deaths in front of the king with their, "It should have been you..." last words.

Father tiptoes over pulseless peers to cry himself to sleep with continually-cheated-of-fun tears.

A new town taking its time.

From everything.

As mother's father flips through the wanted ads, mother watches a none-too-much-older girl in this roadside diner pulling strings of steam from a coffee cup. Gooey strands like sleep from the eyes of dreamers spending Spring days under tin roofs waiting for rain... the very time stripped from liquid; a manipulation forcing it to cool.

And, as children do, mother asks the obvious, "Why'd you did that?"

And, as children who only know to repeat the things adults do and say, the girl replies with not enough veracity, "To prove Time has no sway over me."

Other patrons pull smoke from the air to grow cigarettes from butts into full fags, finally flaring a blackened match into a pristine piece of wood to light both again to burn away one more one last time. Subtle until noticed.

It is only a novelty to the new family. With mother's parents watching in periphery, mother's siblings mimic the trick on hot cocoas without success.

This is a city without work for a bridge builder. Everyone happily believes they are beyond Time so none feel the need for manufactured shortcuts. Not a one thinking She treats them like inanimate objects each time eyes close. No. All believe themselves beyond the need for a softstone bedroom floorbridge where the bed dangles from suspension wires, leaving aged indentations of sand footprints whenever She comes calling... sinking in the soft rock just enough to leave the sleeper out of reach.

And, from fear of becoming equally deluded, mother immediately decides never to take up smoking or twirling fingers over steaming cups.

The smells of home travel everywhere.

Lighter than a lunchbox or backpack, father carries cigarette smoke to the first day of school as an unknown burden. A simple indicator of class. Separated at schoolhouse doors into the majority: factory workers and potential stars of conference league sports.

Father finds this fortunate, quickly learning recess is the reward for always answering with a "Yes, ma'am." Or a "Yessir."

The few learning to read watch from malicious windows overlooking the blacktop games as chalkboards scrape with mundane ways to manipulate this acquiescent world.

1.7

Something like home is made in another new town.

Some waterless desert landscape demanding bridges for someday rains. A contract to span every empty concrete canal and sandtrap moat surrounding the more expansive homes. All slated to be built within five years.

And, given the opportunity, mother's family seeks the normality others have: mother's father works nine-to-five; mother's mother attempts domesticity in a long-term leased house; mother and mother's sister wake early weekday morns to walk roads that drop into dipping someday waters to attend the schoolhouse where mother marvels at the incomprehensible speech of the gawking students staring at mother's comparatively pale skin.

Little time spent away from a silent family left much of the world incomprehensible.

This is a holiday mother's family does not celebrate. Let loose from school as parades stutter at bridges not yet built, mother watches mother's father draw drawbridges into mudbrick walls with a chisel and chains while these sounds overlap with unknown jubilations coming from these unknown people. And this juxtaposition of familiar and unknown is one of those defining moments with unknown consequences.

In this moment mother chooses the familiar.

In this moment mother renounces all unknown.

Nights never hold sleep here.

There are just some towns where the sun tires its occupants and its absence is relished. Or maybe people within look better at night and it is exhausting to try to remember how attractive they can be in the light of day. Or, maybe, the opposite can be true: the smell of a woman's skin after the right amount of time in the sun can be as close to perfection as most men will ever find so all life is lived at night to avoid circumstances creating constant longing.

Whichever. Father's hometown is none of these things. They know what the mill on the hill takes from them and they, the never-rested, sacrifice unwanted waking lives for those they possess in sleep. These majority holdouts listen for shift change whistles and nap in the broken increments of the only things theirs.

In father's home, night harbors employment.

Father's father works the mill overlooking town; an empty orchestra of men and machines trying to mill the memories of this town's denizens into compartmentalized commodities to be exported to places in need of such lonely lives.

Father's mother works the bars and their patrons, trying for more than a buzz before the anticipated 05.00 whistle alerts the town to a marriage bed return.

Father's brother and father employ child-sized ulcers through these weekday nights. Too worried their house will be the one place in town where something new will happen. Most nights, father's mother stumbles in an hour before the shift-change whistle whittles away at the town and sleep is found in the cracks of snooze stricken alarming clocks.

Then there are the other weekdays: whistle wailing its way into father's motherless house like an Olympic gunshot and racing home unseen is impossible to do on one-lane streets. So father's brother and father get ready for school. Too young to shave and too terrified to shit, each shower then dress in turn and wait for the bus hours before it or the

1.10

sun is due to arrive. Inevitably, father's mother spins tires through a field or in the gaps between neighbors' houses to beat father's father home by seconds. These days, they are the only children in the world who dress before sleeping: both nodding off upright in school bus seats, desks and bleachers. The mill taking everything they stayed awake trying to keep.

The clouds of mother's youth commit.

Not so indecisive to trickle a drop at a time. Never the namby-pamby claims of "Chance of precipitation..." that will later be crapshoot predicted.

Mother spends isolated after-school days climbing trees to catch these clouds. Here, if a cloud decides to be a disemboweled rabbit, it is a disemboweled rabbit until death. No subtle shifts to minotaur to basket of fruit and bacon fat to barbed-wire wrapped corpse... each remains dedicated to perfecting one form.

And they never fall without cause.

Sometimes they are tripped by mountains or wind or power lines, drug down by a child in a tree or shot by a farmer watering the fields. Or, sometimes, they fall for comedy. Mother's mother films mother, six years old, climbing down from a failed attempt to catch a cloud with the family's new 8mm. As feet touch green ground and mother shrugs at the one that got away, the out-of-reach cloud falls from the sky. A large pond or a small lake in the guise of a trunkless elephant tumbling down in one downpour. The soon-to-be ruined camera documents mother's face falling open, gasping then fading to crackled static before showing the expression settled upon: a sob or a smile.

Probably a smile, though. Mother appreciates the humor of clouds.

Behind the empty koi pond is the garden.

Father's neighbor Don has no fence around it, neither scarecrows nor a rocking chair to sit shotgun waiting to ward away intruders. There's no need. Everything placed in the ground rises to show its appreciation. Mainly green beans and tomatoes. And, if anyone is paying attention, the crops climb a bit higher the closer they grow to father's window.

But there are accidental crops, too.

Father left his bike in a hurry, skidded into the ground, and it is now the exposed root structure of a rubber tree plant.

Winged scavengers carried rocky mountain oysters from the chopping-block-fields and hid them in the garden for another day, giving rise to hairy stalks that sprout phalli flowers of indecorous aromas.

Even Old Man Hendricks took to burying things there. The day after she died, he buried his wife behind the beets. The felt-flesh flowers blooming there resemble the narcissus in the faded hue of Mrs. Hendricks' complexion but they wilt without fertilization; as barren in death as in life.

And there are things that came by unknown means: a turntable tree plays the indentation of wind with its thorns, shoestring vines strangle their way up the old elm, venus fastfood-Styrofoam-container-traps hang their logo-adorned lids open in anticipation of cheeseburgers.

But the beer bottles were no accident. Don's wife forbidding the sins of alcohol so a new crop of lagers are planted each year; green and brown glass bushes flowering tin cap flowers. Every evening, outside father's bedroom window, Don is seen breaking brittle limbs off of bushes. Bleeding lips speak silent gratitude, drinking up everything the ground has to offer. Walking inside each night to proclaim, "I cannot get rid of those damned weeds."
There's an uncle in the hills behind every new town.

Hidden from the world until another barrel of excess

moonshine can be traded for the materials to make eight more. It is possible they were all afflicted with the James Dean-esque reckless beauty of mother's father. At one time. Now they are jug blowers, baritone whistlers in the depleting liquid happiness... trying to emulate the sound an exhausted sigh makes in the barrel of a shotgun. A call of, "Here Deathie, Deathie, Deathie Death! Come here, Deathie! That's a good Death! Who's my good Death? Is it you? Yes it is!"

Mother met them each by accident.

2.12

It could have been the train tracks

Sometimes they scream.

Depending upon the load and speed, sometimes they simply moan. Sure.

But, sometimes, they scream. Corners taken too quickly leaving cars unsure of their ability to hold onto this world. That is the scream: inanimate objects preparing for the other world. These noises can be heard from indeterminate distances; from living room to as far as the state line at times.

Same screams can sometimes happen when vagrants give too much adventure to the youths who thought they were ready for it.

At seven, father knows all of these lullaby screams.

Tonight, it comes from the basement where the train does not go. This is where all the town's families keep their most vocal mistakes. Father clears away the closet-hidden benign: a Plinko game box; outgrown Sunday clothes unworn since the one Sunday father's mother found and lost religion; crumpled Monopoly money; fetuses of future skeletons; knickknacks and trinkets from places father has yet to see. Beneath them is the trapdoor to the bomb shelter basement.

Beneath the trapdoor is the one universality of all basements: the smell. From dirt floors to refurnished posh underground apartments with pink tiled showers, all smell the same. Other than that? Little more in father's childhood basement resembles any other, other than dirt and empty space between disturbing things. Thousands of them. Stacked on shelves, nailed to walls, suspended from the floorboards by magnets and meathooks. There are even a few glass cases sitting upon royal purple velvet... the most disturbing things are, often, the greatest accomplishments.

This is how father came to know father's parents: nightly following screams to their silent stories untold by adults in daylight and hidden from the mill that would mold them into anything benign.

By morning, the board games and tarnished trinkets are back in their proper places of chaotic rest that look impossible to move in the course of one night. Mornings leave father forever questioning the veracity of secrets disguised as somnambular hallucinations.

Uncle #1:

Mother is lost. Another after-school day alone, this one spent following flying insects across flat horizons in all directions. Darkness comes quickly beneath the immutable clouds of mother's youth so the old man hunched on an older white mare goes unnoticed until the distance is too close to avoid cordiality. Now mother notices notable features: sunken face with attractive features closely resembling mother's father, a fallen-shoulder-posture perfect for dive bar barstools substituted by the mare and the oft-lifted jug. And they trade the familiar "Hello"s of distant family, showing this uncle inherited a more talkative nature than mother's father, gesturing a gentle offering of the jug with, "Would you like any, my niece?"

"No. Thank you, good uncle, but no. I'm lost and wondering if you could...?" ended by the sound in the jug raised to old lips that dry too quickly. A sound unknown to the young.

"What was that?"

"Moonshine, my dear niece. And there's no need to refer to it in the past tense, there's plenty left." Raised again in offer.

"No. Thank you again, good uncle, but no. I meant the noise."

"Oh. This?" On queue, the demon within tries to escape by beating a beaten head against the clay vessel.

"Yes. That."

"Dear niece, there are a thousand ways to construct a death rattle. Your father didn't get all the engineering know-how in the family. I can build bridges just as well as him."

"Can father, then, build death rattles as well as you?"

The old man lets loose mother's father's familiar smile while stating, "Yes, dear niece. He built some of the best."

With that, mother quickly remembers her original query in the blackness that fell in the course of conversation. Asking the black-on-black silhouette of mother's father's mounted brother, "Could you tell me the way home?"

"No, niece," is spoken while descending the decrepit beast, walking closer to add, "But this old mare still has one return left in her." Then, after helping mother into the saddle, finishes with, "Just let loose of the reins."

And it was true. The old mare did not let loose a rattle of her own until the morning after it carried mother home.

Father follows father's father to the mill.

Family days let sons know where they will someday be sacrificing backs and lifetimes. Tours telling tales as ghosts of lost limbs linger with the onlookers watching everything almost-known as it is milled into a pulp.

Every first kiss. Every thought of escape. Every hand first held. Every show tune jingle. Every orgasm. Everything worth doing in the operating hours of this near-nonstop draining workshop. Every one taken so it feels almost new the next time, and a little less the next, and a little less, and a little less. Until the not-taken things have no novelty at all and the general assumption is that it has all been done before.

1.10

All on display before being packaged but none look. The town survives on this one industry alone and watching what it does would inspire arson in the time between shifts.

When there is no more screaming machinery to walk around, they file through the far more terrifying lunchroom illustrating that the slave labors of men are not even given an illusion of comfort or freedom until short-lived weekends. Then it's off to end on a positive note: father and all other children are handed portentous kites to fly in the turbulence of smokestacks.

The heat disembowels some. Nothing but the stick frame playing out the actions expected; swaying and jettisoning in disparate directions, learned movements kept up out of habit.

A few break at the string. Either spiraling into the foreverness of overcast or choosing gravity over propulsion to tumble into the smokestacks with an incinerated flare.

But most stay intact, pulling for freedom while little hands withhold it for entertainment.

Father's kite is one of the first: disemboweled.

Mother's becomes a life of voices.

Another violation of the things that define mother's parents. But it is not mother's voice. She is enamored by them because she does not possess the ability to say these things forever gone unheard.

A brand new transistor radio the only thing as portable as a bridge builder's family. Tiny speakers speaking understandable words in those years hidden in a silent home surrounded by incomprehensible surroundings. Always tucked beneath mother's head like an ear-born tumor singing poppy lessons of love and lost love and first love and unrequited love and perfect love gone wrong and loved ones dying or leaving or...

No different now as the wood-paneled station wagon leaves another town unhappy. This one discontented with the pace of progress, believing the bridges will never be done in time for the antediluvian world to come.

Mother listens to promises made across airwaves justifying the belief that the new place could be better than the last.

Always East.

West reveals mountains and an ocean but father's parents' family live on the other side of eternal flatlands so summers are airconditionless weeks of driving with a fighting sibling and bickering parents never hiding the fact being amidst family is always a mistake. All for a four-day stay with strangers strapped with the same last name.

Father survives by anticipating the next rest stop stuck between state lines. Impossible to tire of standing in two places at once in the glass shops filled with gimcracks of glazed plates and key chains making the soon-to-be-seen-again monuments feel monumental by being worthy of being re-rendered in miniature.

Out here, every memory is the property of those that commit them.

And father loves the identical motels: three stories stacked in a square where numbered doors face out to a rectangular pool. Father's brother simply swims and ignores the intricacies father, since six until now at nine, organizes: Shark, Tag, Marco Polo. A displaced, aquatic refugee camp filled with ever-present groups of girls giggling in the shallow end, ready to play.

All done for the unmentionable thrill of wrinkly fingers coming in contact with another's flesh.

Somehow, the medium of water makes touching a stranger's barely-clad bare skin socially acceptable. Addicting long beyond the hours permitted. The girls leave one by one for a towel, then a numbered room where someone yells their name as extinguished lights let father fall into the water's forever darkness.

1.4

The universality of peers escapes mother.

Too well illustrated in this new school tucked in the shadows of towering buildings where mother's father can be seen atop each during the day, building sky bridges so the rich never have to touch the deathly streets of peasants. Here, mother's patched accent and silent clothes transcend any accepted norm so eight hours of a waking life is lived alone among thirty others in a room. They should be similar. All taught the same imported words, arithmetic, first experiences, state capitols, jingles from sitcoms, commercials and cartoons.

But in this world mother was made for, she fits it very poorly.

It was most obvious at night. Another new town of children dreaming universal dreams to be replayed beyond relevance: forgetting locker combinations and class schedules, unprepared and late for tests, pantsless hallway walking while teeth fall from terrified faces.

Mother does not dream from this common well.

Mother dreams in diagrams and line drawings, sharp angles and two dimensions. All silent.

This is why mother will never fit into the unconstructed world. Not due to a perceived individualistic unconscious: everyone believes their dreams to be as unique as they believe themselves to be. No, mother's isolation comes from believing her uniqueness is universal.

Father likes the road noise.

Head against a concussive window causing open eyes to jar and jettison reality into, if not something better, something tolerably different.

But there is none of that tonight.

Nor are there rest stops or motels.

It is a speedometer-ignored drive listening to the radio as father's mother wrings hands in rhythm with a shaking head. It's hard to hear the details as crackles distort the exact measurements of the catapult or the ship's name it is built upon or how the bow is holding up. The only thing that is always heard is the continual countdown raising the moon from the horizon to within range.

Father's father nay-says in, "Just you wait..." and, "Mark my words..." predictions of devastation.

But all eyes watch it rise in the East. Top crescent of the full moon seen and witnessed with the knowledge everything will be different tomorrow.

But there is road noise between the final descending numbers.

The car swerves during the indeterminate countdown as all eyes fix on the radio, forever longer than ten seconds, believing it will reveal more than the orb rising in front of them. Only abandoning it with the words, "We have lift-off!"

Then the known world witnesses it, all simultaneously. A hole in the papier-mâché face of the moon.

Father's father, minutes later, finally mustering a:

– *What'd I tell you?*

Not all the known world watches.

A misstatement. Mother is the one exception, bathtub soaking in a windowless room made for escaping petty concerns like those of the moon as miniature bubbles fill newfound crevices in skin. Mother chooses the familiar over the broadcast of the unknown.

In another world, a room designated for living, mother's family watches a television instead of sticking heads outside; a medium of fiction mediating images of dubious veracity. And it is this format, surely, that allows them to laugh as the man puts a larger-than-man-sized hole in the satellite. A parody of expectations in that forever fall.

It takes the somber tone of commentators to make it feel real. All with their:

– *Our prayers go out to the family of astronaut Neil Armstrong.*
and mother hears mother's father's:

– *It never would've happened had they built a bridge...*
but none put words to the true concern.

Night will never have the mystery it once did as all the world feels newly unknown.

Sports find father in middle school.

Each an aptitude test for manually laboring life away: football; wrestling; track. Nine months of contradictory commands screamed in indecorous ways:

– *Don't let that bastard run by you!*

– *Don't run from your opponent!*

– *Run, you son of a bitch, run!*

The only measure of success is complete obedience without questioning. It should be winning but this town's teams have been running the same sequence of plays since the mill was founded, so only obedience can be measured.

The logical responses never occur to father. Never thinking to ask:

– *Why play four complete quarters if the fourth is the only one worth watching?*

– *Why not agree to sideline sit until there are only ten minutes left?*

– *Why must adolescent boys wear awkwardly tight school-colored spandex while throwing or being thrown around by other adolescent boys?*

– *Why put obstacles in the way of running?*

This is father's schooling: a life of structured performance within illogically confining rules.

But there is consolation in being built for this world.

As everyone tries to acclimate to being built for afterlives, mother lives with a contented sense of purposelessness; built for nothing more than this senseless place.

In the beginning, mother attempted to make schoolyard friends with those girls who believed they were made in the image of the divine. Inevitably, these attempts failed. Their vaguely known deities never gave reasons why this world failed a visage of immortality. Still, these prissy demigods demand worship.

Built for this world of practical things, mother cannot grasp the demands of the irrational. Incapable of offering frankincense and myrrh compliments to wardrobe choices, impossible to offer self-deprecating sacrifices in the image of them. Inevitably asking:

– *Why?*

Learning for the first and only time that no one enjoys their purposeful lineage questioned.

This morning, father's mother doesn't make it home in time.

At the sunrise bus stop, father and father's brother fearfully watch the garage door only reveal an electric light in its rise. Watching father's father's car not pulling inside, an idling observation of the vacant space. Watching shoulders fall an instant before the face and— even from that distance —an instantaneous onset of aging is seen— no longer needing oceans.

Inexplicably, father's father cautiously pulls forward. Parks. Walks— a brokenness of steps not even the mill could inspire —inside, beating the oncoming train by an unsafe margin, in an attempt to find normalcy.

1.4

Uncle #2:

Mother takes the wrong trolley, trying to too-quickly escape the escapades of school. Already eight stops away before realizing the error, watching city streets to see which is the best to step into. All alike. All filled with standing or stoop-sitting men pulling brown bags from each other to pull from.

Then it is seen: familial traits etched in a stranger's face who sat on a red ice box alone. Jumping from the moving object with an all too excited:

– *Uncle!*

turns a dozen nearby men to study mother's features, seeking a trickle of a familial stream. All others turn away, leaving mother's father's brother to acquiesce to the likeness.

– *Hello, niece. To which of my brothers should you be returning?*

Mother says mother's father's name while listening carefully for whatever sounds the raised brown bag may make— but hears nothing.

– *Ah, yes. Thought that was his handiwork littering the skyline.*

Hesitantly, more to fill the silence between them disturbing the cacophonous street than wanting an answer, mother asks:

– *Are you a builder, too, dear uncle?*

Mother's father's brother smiles that patrilineal smile as a group of men tentatively approach with soft spoken words:

– *Got any more of that stuff for us?*

and mother's father's brother shifts from the cooler, pulls out another brown bagged bottle and hands it off to the eager eight. Explaining to mother as they fight over its contents:

– *Yes, child. I am a builder, too. Death traps are my specialty. Bottled wood and springs, mostly, preserved in formaldehyde.*

Now the one who had the bottle is being beaten with it. No longer moving as blood forgets which side of skin it belongs on.

    – *Then father can build death traps too?*

    – *Quieter ones. Patienter ones. But death traps, all the same.*

Unsettled, mother finally asks:

    – *Can you tell me the way home?*

    – *I could send you to your final home a thousand different ways... but where you live? No, I cannot help with that.*

Said while gesturing to a bus heading the way mother came, returning to a place closely resembling home.

Father stays after wrestling practice.

Asks coaches to explain a throw again, lifts weights, sprints toward vomiting; diversions from the blood and screams inevitably decorating furniture, floorboards and walls by now. At the age of twelve, the inevitability of home is an inevitable return— but can still be delayed until excuses exhaust themselves.

Walking now in the similar light of sunset reveals nothing changed: father's father's parked truck parked next to nothing but an oil stain.

Inside sits father's wrinkled father— brown hair silvered, eyes dulled, strong hands strung thin on swollen joints sewn together with exposed and scattered veins —flipping through the same five network channels. Father avoids asking the unanswerable, settling for:

– Dad? What are you doing home?

Responding in a nasal voice assaulted by the fear of age:

– They retired me today.

Then, upon examining father, father's father follows up with:

– Hey, get in the truck.

– Where we goin'?

– Lookin' for Mother.

From the passenger seat, father watches as the old Chevy tours town bars— slowing at each to let old eyes focus on parking lot parked cars. Nothing. Nothing but the recognition that father's father already knew; always knew. So the tour is made again, father's father saying at each:

– Go on in there and ask if they've seen her.

as every bartender answers a variation of:

– No, not since night before last.

Both aged some as the truck pulls into the center of the garage; one tire on each oil stain. Doors slam shut. In this moment— waiting on the train to pass before entering the kitchen —father watches departing children a year or three older, waving goodbyes, and rethinks the inevitable.

Mother's father decides to build a son.

True to form, never speaking reasons. To pass on a knowledge of building or the loneliness among a world of women? An accidental whimsy of the moment? Someday slave labor? Maybe only now had mother's mother abandoned hope of retaining once-was beauty and acquiesced to gifting halved features again?

That's the thing with silent people: no one knows.

Either way— after nine months of labor —mother has a new brother and takes to filling the crib with Lincoln Logs and Legos, toothpicks and superglue— ready to witness what death-related patrilineal traits might be avoided or exploited.

2.3

Father and father's brother age, too.

Father's brother now is finished with school and finishes six-packs of beer after each new day at the mill with a:

– *Let me tell you about my day...*

air; never saying a thing, though. Each laboriously earned memory milled away with the rest to make the anticipation of another day possible.

Father cooks microwave meals and serves everyone from two-liter cylinders of soda. No one cleans. Father's father and father's brother forget their age— when mirrors become deceptive, what use are calendared dates to rely upon? —and become lost to peers; Time set the course for these disjointed lives long ago. Not knowing who their peers are makes evenings void of everyone but each other; not knowing how to act in a way appropriate to expectations. So these two men are watched by father, unavoidable warnings, as they watch television for anything distracting enough to be entertaining.

1.1

It takes two months, but mother's predictions are true:

The new sibling is a prodigy.

Not one of any import; Legos and Lincoln Logs found their way to factory suggested forms— down to the alternating colors —as everything else went untouched.

To see if it is a matter of hues, mother deposits a discombobulated Rubik's cube into the crib and it is left alone; already in its meant-to-be form.

So the crib-built structures are shaken for any rattle then tentative fingers prod to see what might trap them inside— but nothing. The most cosmetic of family traits inherited: pretty structures without purpose. Perhaps mother's mother sacrificed more of herself on this one than anyone realized.

Girls come as a rediscovery.

Every girl already known; explored in forgottenly milled grade school moments— while babysat at some neglectful home, possibly his own, or at school behind wallball walls or inside the jungle gym or after the bell— a flash of cartoon decorated panties —while panicked adults sought them out.

And maybe it was a gradual progression— them getting like this.

Or maybe it all happened the summer before this first day of high school.

These bodies resemble nothing of the once-were explored. Cracked and crawled from three month shells to reveal these impossibly firm representations of almost women.

Somehow it makes father resent father's mother more instead of acknowledging the lust other men had for her. No. A confused wondering of:

– *Why?*

But father's mother never looked this good.

1.14

The riots topple mother's father's work.

Bringing bridges down to ground level so no one can escape anyone else. A true revolution seems imminent for a minute; all with its:

– *Death to the enablers of the rich!*

slogans uprooting mother's family again. It would have gone on forever; all wealth stolen and distributed, all mankind linked and loved— but the wealthy always have backup plans. They long ago purchased copyrights to words like: revolution, expropriations, anarchy, riots, bourgeoisie, death, etc. Earning a penny per use per printed issue and copyright infringement if spoken without expressed written consent.

The revolution© funds their ascent again.

Mother's father doesn't say it as they drive through molotoved streets burning, but mother knows it is sibling rivalry; one brother's death traps trumping the work of the other.

Every generation needs a war.

And it is not that the war does not want father's participation— simply born too late; straggling behind that collection of near-peers. So— before winter break —father watches a new batch of boys board buses, dice-rolling to see which will return corpses and which will return spent casings from bullets sent survivalist directions.

Most forgotten until newspapers list those arranged letters which will soon be etched in stone. Small towns have a way of producing such similar creatures that it hardly seems to matter to the girls left behind. Father is enough like any other boy to tend the needs of the abandoned.

Perhaps it is a matrilineal blood-born pathogen; an engrained adherence to the physical needs of others without concern for much else. If that is the case, father inherits this dynasty well— rediscovering each in their turn, many in some of the same games: doctor, hide and seek in the dark, schoolyard teases.

Whichever, everyone in every generation needs a war, and father will need to find a new war to supplant the one missed.

1.15

Mother morphs in the backseat.

Rest stop mirrors incrementally reveal hips breaking wide with blood, chest swelling beyond the cover of hunkered shoulders— the rearview mirror hints at a woman's body that may be more beautiful than those that built it.

Somehow, mother's family doesn't seem to notice.

This is not something they constructed.

2.7

They quickly become tiresome.

These known girls who— beyond any amount of milling could cover —have known too many boys.

All offering flashbacks to father's mother if father had known father's mother then— Oedipal obsessions as properly disturbing as they should be. In a town this small, all features overlap in unflattering ways.

And don't they become tiresome after the first time? Never a surprise. Not that it stops father from continually seeking— but it's as though they were all taught the same mechanical moves as a whole.

Or maybe the whole town knows new things are built by the mill milling old things in unique ways and this exploration of the new should be left to those employed to make such dangerous decisions. This act of creation is safe if only done in old ways.

Or maybe they all secretly believe anything creative will become the new norm, taken when the mill inevitably employs them to be manufactured and sent abroad; highest bidders obtaining these positions and emotions— safest if they all remain possibilities locked in masturbatory imaginations.

Or maybe it is the thing father refuses to consider— not the fault of girls but boys. Imagination battling execution in arenas where there are no coaches, timeouts or substitutes.

Whichever, father tires of things done while still in the act of doing them.

1.14

A truly unremarkable place.

Mother's infant brother finding work before mother's father; framing future houses with fanatical zeal. Cubes of Rubikless charm indicating any aesthetic would need to be taught in this place where people only escape without the help of bridges.

So mother's father erects models— miniatures of the best miracles —to display to the city council, district officials, wealthy patrons; trying to build anything resembling another life as mother mirror-watches everything new, feeling for the first time that this body was not built and owned by someone else. No— for a moment —mother knows this was her willing creation.

Then the whistle blows, mindless men go back to work and...

2.5

There is talk of new inhabitants in father's town.

Which is to say there is not talk of anything else. The town's first strangers— tales told of misplaced accents, odd occupations and, most importantly, two sisters near father's age. Just like the rest of town— no, more time taken than the rest of town; escaping home in search of this something new —father spends the winter break patrolling streets in anticipation of a happenstance encounter. Only seeing mother's mother in the supermarket, thinking:

   – I'll bet she was once beautiful...

thoughts.

This, the first day in mother's last school.

The second day of a new year because this is back when years became new again. Maybe it helps people become anew, too. Mother walks familiarly unfamiliar hallways—memorizing new names and locker combinations —as popular senior girls introduce themselves and marvel that mother is only a sophomore.

All the boys stare.

Mother is ready for any sensationally new sensation to finally happen in this new body.

2.7

we

they

Mother is no better built than the girls already here.

But father and other boys do not care; all want to discover for themselves if this unknown mother is put together in the ways already witnessed in truck beds and stolen magazines.

The wind is the only thing brave enough to take the initiative— pressing the sun dress against her body on the hood of a Chevy outside the Taste-E-Treat. A new smile infects small towns with the promise of an elsewhere life; new bodies— if beautiful —do so much more than smiles. This is the proof there is no need to inherit the promised beauty of parents.

So mother fearfully refuses offered cigarettes from the girls and greets each unknown suitor with a giggle and a concealed smile; the only surefire response learned in all schools attended. Maybe it is because father is familiarly awkward— six months younger and a grade behind with a newly wrestling-season-shaved head —or maybe it is just chance that places mother on father's hood— a simple 1 in 8 parking spots chance that makes father's already-old Chevy the closest as mother needs to make it back to fourth period.

Maybe mother will not become methodical until much later. Maybe this happenstance, in the face of so many others, was coincidentally familiar in a world soon never to be.

Or maybe it is this awkwardness that mother finds familiar.

The newness of another inspires insanities.

Delusions of belief conjuring constructed people better than they are.

So— this night after first meeting —mother and father imagine the person each of them could be with this other someone; neither realizing how little they like themselves until imagining how different someone different could make them. For the first time, father sees a future man who can do something other than work a life away at a mill while a wife does indecorous things at home; mother sees a life lived in one stable place.

Inevitably, little things change about them both.

The same things.

Both smile more often; both forgive and forget the sins of parents and siblings; both lose track of time and obligations. But most notable: their narration is no longer singular— neither can think of themself individually.

3.14

Father earns a varsity jacket the following year.

Mother adds it to a wardrobe attuned to a half-dozen other school colors. The contrast speaks loudly, letting everyone know in complimentary colors that mother is taken. Always wearing it but, especially, to Fall football games; pulling arms inside and tucking knees within— engulfed by the name strung to father that the town shouts from the bleachers behind.

Already it feels more right attached to mother than it ever did on father— a thing gifted to anyone willing to wear it — further proving this body was not the manufactured thing of youth.

3.7

They talk of someday actualities.

Both from a generation promised a great deal of inevitable things by forty: flying cars, deep sea colonies, robotic friends, cures for cancer and the common cold, apocalypses avoided. So— in the context of life —forever promises seemed assured.

    – We will always be together.
    – We will always love each other.
    – We will always feel just like this.
They never knew we were coming.

3.5

(temporal)

They make it through high school as most do—

Making love in the back of automobiles, breaking up in morning then back together by lunch, father fighting some other boy over mother in the parking lot as mother and the school watch in exalted anxiety.

Mother graduates first, just before mother's father— only able to find work building the banal with mother's brother —moves the family away again. Father gives a ring left behind by father's mother and mother stays behind like a ring; getting a job at an arctic themed fast food place where the secret sauce ingredients are given away on the first day— another misplaced word. Here letterman jackets mean nothing as the degrading theme of a place that rarely sees snow has entrees of polar bear burgers, penguin nuggets and glacier ice in flavors of "blue" and "red".

Father still lives in the world where wearing one's own letterman jacket signals availability. And father's ties to father's mother may be stronger than any name strewn anywhere— partaking in the variously named fruits— Cindy, Jenny, Jennifer, Jen, Tiffany —allowed to a sports star in an illiterate town; names chosen in the constant consideration of mother. Each sounding similar enough to the name that feels like home so that, if moaned at inopportune times, it can be plausibly called irrational jealousy if noticed.

3.14

Uncle #3:

Father meets this soon-to-be in-law— the only one present —and listens to things said, follows them with an:

– I do.

two months after graduation.

Father's brother wheels in father's decrepit father— the only other family in attendance. And, as youth are apt to do, they replicate the norms of weddings: wedding cake in the face, money dances, talking in tongues. Father drinks with long-known acquaintances and indiscriminately watches the women in the room it is now a sin to touch; mother finds a moment to speak with mother's father's brother, asking:

– Do you do this often? Marriages?

– Yes, niece.

– Then I've finally met someone in the family capable of building situations for life!

And mother's father's brother smirks— a full smirk, with its half smile and condescending exhalation exhaled loud enough to be heard —examining the perceived faulty craftsmanship of siblings.

– No, child. Situations, perhaps. Yes. Let us say I build situations where people will always wish for the things they do not have in life.

– Wishes in opposition to life? You are a builder of death wishes, then.

said without surprise or disgust; family will do as family does.

– Is father, then—?

No need to finish, mother watches father's learned behavior for a response.

They park the green truck— shaving cream stained in:
  – *JUST MARRIED!*
formations eating into the paint —in the same parking spot where they met.

Dining on ice cream cones, they watch soon-to-be high school kids who do not know or care they are in the presence of The New Girl and The Three Sport Letterman. No. All these children simply run around, obsessed with themselves.

Then to the drive-in theater they always went to—

Then to the tiny apartment mother had lived in since mother's family left—

Nothing different, really, save that— come morning — father will follow father's father's footsteps to the mill.

3.2

As expected, the first day goes forgotten.
   And the next.
   And the next.
   And father slowly realizes— coming home this three-hundredth first day of work to a wife showing and a hairline falling further back —that father's father lived a lifetime like this: one long post-war day doing nothing memorable... wondering what may have stood out in such a life.

3.10

Some nights, father escapes the newly pregnant new bride.

AWOL in the chosen war: domestic life. Never needing a medal, father suffers duties silently in the faint hope of enjoying these nights where the few surviving acquaintances return from the war of father's generation— none displaced... or aged. Men return unlike any in father's father's time; they are returning excused.

Leaving, they raised right hands and swore to protect everything loved from all threats, foreign and domestic.

Returning, they raise left hands timidly— asking:

– *Please, Ms. Life? May I be excused?*

as She writes hall passes for them to bypass sanity and other unwanted burdens.

And the laughter.

Father sits with faces much like those starring in high school memories— but the laughter is off. Not the contagious laughter of father's father. No. This is laughter to laugh along with— all who hear it know to chuckle and nod —because it is fearful of what will take its place if it ever stops.

So first sips are spilled on sticky floors and even a new wife— with girth threatening to forever alter father's world —seems great to go home to by closing time.

3.15

Father hears the:
  – *Congratulations!*
over the mill intercom.

Mother was well prepared for the occasion but father entered the forever workday as a married man and is today leaving a family man. It makes the necessity of a bar found— celebrating for four days in an imploding world before finding home to greet the suspicious offspring.

we

we

we

she

81

she is not to blame.

born a month later, sure— but cut from the dying world of the last mother. a survival instead of a birth.

the second surprise being she needed assistance in getting that first scream out; slapping, prodding, starved. held as a refrigerated incubator captive until it finally shattered from the face of she.

it came as Pandora's last gift came: expected for failed reasons.

5.19

we moved into a four-room green house without walls.

a new family under a roof held up by two screen doors, all surrounded by a white picket fence also engulfing two trees curled and growing downward in the front yard; another in back doing the same. down the road to the South was a cul-de-sac, to the North was town.

the neighbors all had walls and curtains to hide the things they did. but we? we were exposed; a sense of decency forced on people too young to conform to forced things.

within the walls that weren't there was little to look at: two bedrooms, one bathroom and a petite kitchen/dining room/television room crammed together in that tiny tiny unresolved hardwood floor plan. even the fireplace had no walls: a hollowed pit in the middle of the room. no need to lean wood against each other to be ignited; at that time we were close enough to Hell to dig down for warmth. mother would scrape away the ash with a third-hand andiron set— maybe they were clawing their way up, too, for the coldness we had in abundance.

and now the idea of bills is absurd; a collection for things that sustain in this unsustainable world. but it was the remnants of the old world we were brought into, and the fire pit provided refuge from one more mother and father couldn't pay.

still, we never should have heated the house that way.

demons snuck in at night. tinier than you would think, no larger than words— so only those with souls were susceptible to their influence. subtly delivered. mock whistling wind thru pretend windows whispering:

– *I was happier without you.*

and the cupboard hinge creaking:

– *I hate you.*

and bathtub drain sucked and slurped:

– *You ruined my life.*

and these first-learned words were replicated in high-volume conversations with each other that echoed off the walls of other neighborhood homes.

father's mother returned.

a wrinkled version of crinkled photos father had to excavate from rubbish bins. well dressed for the assumed role of grandmother given without deliberation or casting calls for other interested parties. not a word said of places seen and father's father did not ask; all treated as one long night waltzing away nights in bars however they once were waltzed away.

so we were often left with aged versions of father's parents while mother and father worked, wading thru cigarette smoke and green shag carpet ten hours at a time. left to memorize soap opera characters and losing to father's mother in chess, chinese checkers, plinko and mousetrap because— in some bar somewhere —the whore learned to cheat. justifying each victory dance with:

– *Be a good loser now. No one likes a crybaby. Loser crybaby...*

4.6

without walls, the house held its inhabitants poorly.

boundaries drawn in malleable mediums: string, chalk, yelled proclamations.

at night, after everyone else found sleep, we inched them askew to reduce the distance between beds; barriers twisted until we all shared one corner of the floor plan. father— waking to piss or silently sneak away from an unwanted life —tripped over another bed before making it as far as the bathroom— cursing shared blood and bed frame edges. threatening to make good on threats if we did not return to pre-sunset boundaries.

it was not the need to feel closer; no one wanted that.

it was an accumulation of the terrifying taken in in a little lifetime: scary movies, news headlines, bedtime stories, baroque music. we knew the world held a grudge after what we did to it.

it was because of that.

we could see the outside world without knowing what it wanted. simple safety in numbers: the closer we slept the more likely It would take someone that wasn't us.

bible study was arts-and-crafts hour.

brought about by father's mother's refound zeal to recant damages done without ceasing them at such a late date— only enforced on major holidays and a handful of sunny days.

too young to be tortured with an hour's worth of sermons, we were hauled into a side room by a woman aged enough to prefer talk of Hell over creating hope in youth. each pupil given a bible. all told to think about the false idols their heathen parents worshiped— then left alone.

so we added water to flour, ripped strips from the books and built papier-mâché constructs of everything we heard our parents pray on/for/between— gas gauges on E, bottles of bourbon, our mothers' legs.

the chewed paper idols filled the room by the end of the hour: another failed pregnancy test, the first infertile patch in a flourishing forty acres, a ringing telephone that won't be picked up because a bill collector could be on the other end— or a forgotten friend that is best forgotten— or a family member telling of death or asking for money— or a...

after all, we worshiped idols in preformed factory plastic figurines— with ready-made mythologies illustrated and presented as an animated morning Mass seen over the lip of a cereal bowl. it seemed unfair for father and mother to be denied the things they prayed for; even if they were embodied in the things they prayed against.

4.17

father could fill a toilet bowl with bubbles.

the entire porcelain-enclosed surface area.

the little magic left in this world was spelled out by adults as explainable facts: cars contained combustion engines, lift was possible by air passing faster under an airplane's wing and slower over it, leap years did not create a day but compensated for the solar system's asymmetry by adding one day to a calendar year every four years unless that year is divisible by 100 and not also divisible by 400.

facts: all we were ever told.

and the fact was that father filled the toilet bowl with bubbles every morning. seat and lid left lifted while showering and dressing; left while leaving for work as tho it was a proclamation of... something. maybe something for the neighbors to see from afar or maybe a documentation of deterioration: a bubble popping for ever degrading thing suffered in a workday. a placid pool by noon.

we tried to replicate it with squirt guns and milk jugs— with aerosol hairspray and well-aimed shaken champagne. some experiments more successful than others but all left bubbleless entry points of varying sizes. in short, we proved father's fact was something impossible.

it put other facts in perspective: one-ton machines were impossible to set in motion with the effortless movement of an ankle; metal cannot fly; a year is inflexible. they could explain away the magic any which way but it was still magic.

mother ~~was not allowed friends.~~

...had little need for friends after we started school.

but mother needed daily breaks before we were contained in state institutions— father ~~dove away angrily for days at a time~~ industriously worked odd hours silently and father's mother needed some time alone to work older men in the house where we could not always play outside until they finished.

so, product of an isolated youth, mother sought out father's female high school acquaintances; all chosen for their willingness— not ability —to babysit. forcing mother to suffer all things asked: tiring Tupperware parties, infrequent girls' nights out, group visits to bikini waxing spas and rekindling remembered jealousies. each more tolerable than we were.

and we were forced into friendships with their children.

proximity is often all it takes for the young. and we tried, realizing shared traits believed to be unique: swirled hips while urinating together, digging near-deep holes for no reason, throwing rocks. such simple things limit blood from being drawn more than once or twice in a day or evening spent together.

even when mother was there, we were always told:

– *Go play somewhere else.*

while mother mingled with a houseful of unliked people— still preferred —listening to them talk over the bleating lamb in the skillet; that's where mother would often escape to: the kitchen. petting what was left of dinner's wool, telling it:

– *It will all be okay.*

soothing lies we were never told. mother is sentimental like that.

and in those times we were forced to escape the company

of adults, we would challenge the others to follow acts of disobedience— leveraged exploits memorized in mental lists documenting future threats.

still, the worst of it all was spending all that time spent in another home. forced to witness other failed families with their broadcasted fights; hidden within walls, their screams were— verbatim —identical to what we screamed.

it should have been reassuring.

it wasn't.

those screams were the only ties we had— the only interaction separating family from everyone else —and all we had was what everyone else shared.

the world was explained the first day of first grade.

not by lectures attempting to teach the alchemical way letters were read and written— as tho just anyone could use words —but by example.

abandoned by legally obligated guardians into rigidly sterile classrooms where one lonely old woman tried to impart order on twenty-three savages by turning us loose on the playground battlefield with the rest of the school. and we, initially, exhilarated in the chaos: boys running to four square courts, tethered poles and the football field; girls running for jumprope lines, hopscotch squares and gender-segregated circles playing with pretty things snuck from home; remainders intermingling on slides, swings and monkey bars.

but it did not take long to see that freedom was made for the strong.

we were not allowed to play, shoved and kicked away until one of the enormous kids looked at a clock-adorned wrist and whistled— then, all over the blacktop, we were handed the tokens of passage: jumpropes; soccer and red rubber balls; hopscotch stones. all of it. holding them for a few seconds before the bell rang and they all needed to be put away.

we learned half of the lesson: we were the only ones without the support and knowledge to make it in a world that wants only to kill.

we learned we were weak.

but back in the classroom we learned the other half— taught by the gorgeous smile of Mackenzie McFettridge in the center seat of the first row as she looked up from a drawing of people more beautiful than we were. even before knowing what it was we wanted from her, we knew that smile— and anyone it chose to shine upon —would be exempt from the troubles plaguing all others. we learned that, for that, we wanted to be strong.

clothing racks were constructed for play.

some better built than others.

worst were those with branches projected upward; metal trees with cloth leaves impossible to climb or hide within.

and those racks that spun so customers wouldn't waste energy walking around— carousel clockwork congesting its interior —were fun in an obstacle course way, but not perfect.

then the innovation of a forked rack: simply one long row with garments displayed to either side; a lightly top-lit tunnel to scurry thru.

but the best were the Spring bargain racks of discounted sweaters, coats and overcoats— enormous caves encircled by last season's fashion mistakes impeding all light. bigger than bedrooms on the outside, larger than a thousand homes inside.

we spent weeks in those department store labyrinths, hearing other children in its enormity but never seeing any— chasing their trails of lost toys in the undocumented terrain. lawless and free, it terrified adults who never tread where their authority is in question.

we lived off of bubblegum flesh— dried and tasteless — still clinging to the remnants of metal skeletons. we hunted the evil glimmering fluorescent creatures falling thru cracks in the sky with the shadows of hands purging the undesirable.

then— when outside screams of mother and crackling intercom threats of invasion became too much to ignore —we willingly left, leaving behind ripped fingernail trimmings or purple pocket lint or a shoe or whatever else we possessed that could prove to future adventurers we lived free for a time, too.

school days were separate but unequal parts of life.

five days of every five-day week were spent in those concrete walls; impossible that they only lasted the eight hours purported by timepieces. still— looking back on it —those eternal days blend into one general malaise with several highlights of suffering.

learning nonsensical things we tried to apply to everyday life: if twenty-seven divided by three equals the nine times Mackenzie will at last look this way then that means the hour after every lunch recess for the next week of days that popularity might be possible if we keep faces free of father given ~~bruises~~ blessings.

it is true: we were the sum of our school days divided by the imprint of home. some came away from the nine-month century between summers larger than the days could have allowed: epic eight-year-olds. some left less than whole numbers, decimal pointing at their proximity to zero or negative numbers. but we always equaled one; the most unmemorable number— the reason why names were placed beneath class photos.

we chronicled the lives of classmates with apostolic zeal while teachers told parents we had a hard time concentrating in class, told counselors we may need to be medicated, told us how to reduce a fraction nineteen times so there was never the need to listen to the first eighteen— we were geniuses of the periphery with C averages and ongoing mental biographies on the thirty-one most important classmates.

she held her chest as commanded.

feeling the fight in the thing everyone wanted. and this action— occurring every morning where people worshiped at the altar of her —caused lips to carve her face into a smile; all of them refusing to blame the perceived indiscretion of self-worship for the simple fact everyone wished they could feel the same thing.

they were wrong.

it was simply an appreciation of possessing something unique in the world.

some mornings, late in the pledge, it fought frantically and she knew then that it would not always be hers— too strong to always be contained. and she had visions of its fate: lost and broken, limping back to her chest for shelter from everyone tougher than it. sometimes she will shelter it, other times it will be tossed to be broken again so she can take comfort in dominating something everyone once wanted.

but it happened too late: her face already scarred with a forgiven smile the world coveted.

5.14

when we were little?

we played doctor and crafted quack concoctions for unneeded cures— toothpaste and hot water for drowning coughs; hair gel creams rubbed on schoolyard-inflicted bruises; suppository blow dryers for... who knows what those were meant to cure. always in the homes of friends. doctor was a game to be played behind solid walls and bathroom doors blocked by open drawers or wedged chairs.

we played at PhDs of alchemic mastery, defending dissertation interrogations of:

– *What are you kids doing in there?*

with its only retort:

– *Be out in just a minute!*

4.6

she waited for anyone to notice.

counter-displaying body for any doctoral boy to touch.

she said she could hear the cancer growing inside of her—
tainted cells taunting with Cassandra death calls. and she
was checked out by all her brother's friends on the tile top;
touched in remote places while she clenched-chest said:

– No, it is up here. Can't you hear it?
but no one ever did.

each pre-cadaver dissection taking keepsakes she never
wanted to lose until little was left but the beating cancer
only she could hear.

5.18

it was Steve who first stumbled—

stepping on a crack maybe made by some irresponsible sidewalk maker or maybe it was just another thing we fractured when we entered this world. and— as is the nature of these things —Steve's mother fell; a broken back displaying a son's carelessness. luckily she lived, otherwise it would have been more than a six-year stint in juvie— more than the lifetime probation of tending to a crippled image of what Steve's mother might have been.

we cowered at the thought of it— this lingering happening from the old world —on playgrounds, always favoring the dying grass and leaping over sidewalk seams in exaggerated gestures like a drunkard in a hopscotch tournament.

but when walking town— holding mother's hand —we taunted and teased lines with our toes. asking:

– Does it count if the tip of my shoe touches? Because they're too big so it's not like I'm stepping on a crack. It's my shoe. Does that count, mom? Look mom, what about this? This, mom? Does this count?
simply to show we had some sway in the world.

as a recourse, we were forced to be reclusive; left at home— where there was only seamless linoleum and carpet —while mother shopped on tiled floors lit up in incessant fluorescent tubes to allow a focus on threats avoided.

we were rarely brought home anything to be remembered.

father had friends over three nights a year.

always for poker parties. no children or women allowed within wall-less walls until they were all gone— preferably broke. but we had the deck's suicide kings wedged in spokes, riding unlit neighborhood streets until dawn as father bet the literal last dime on a pair of cowboys against three threes.

the luck of the family draw as obscenities and overturned tables were the:

– *See you again soon?*

parting words.

4.6

a gap adding to the age of we since anything was born.

scientists sought explanations by organizing mobs to gather the youngest children in the world. all paraded on reality TV shows— the only thing to compete with nostalgic remakes of old sitcoms —where birth certificates dictated freedom or death. half-hours spent weeding down the contestants from eighteen to two— always ending with a:

– And the youngest contestant is.... going to be announced tomorrow night! Tune in to find out which of these two will be ritualistically slaughtered for the benefit of humanity! See you tomorrow night!

so the next night could be dedicated to sobbing family members saying:

– I always knew it was his fault...

before being burned alive on live television.

mother and father knew it was only a matter of time before we were found— but they never notified the television authorities. on one hand, it was an act of self-sacrifice knowing they would be made season finale stars for a night but we had become tolerably familiar burdens as mother and father forgot how to be together. father had begun to hope we would follow in footsteps that would be engulfed by the shoes we already wore. and mother knew we were what her family always built, true, but always debating if destroying destructive creations would be a creative act in itself.

the ratings died off faster than the world's youth did. it took a few years but— eventually —everyone realized it only mirrored reality in its cruel and depressing demeanor; redundant to live a pathetic life while watching another's for fun.

we never meant to bring down Heaven.

it was just that our after-school couch-cushion fortresses kept requiring the dismantlement of more and more furniture to rival the castles of our neighbors. upward. warring with imaginary weapons repelled by foam— but we had biological intentions within the peace talks. we sent sisters into afghan-draped darkened war rooms to deliver false promises and silent deaths— armed with cooties, runny noses and chlamydia —as their ambassadors lifted dresses to tempt us into the same demise.

no matter how many neighborhood kids we killed off, more came with the comfort of couches, recliners and love seats to raise the patchwork walls of our almost-toppled enemies. it would have gone on forever; every side with the same sized living rooms to ransack— never the advantage of a den or any hope of pilfering the remnants of a garage-stored smoking stool. all sides were equally poor.

a cold war afternoon.

until one side punctured the floor-boards of Heaven.

we didn't do it. all the same, it tumbled into our living rooms at the same instant causing every other fortress to fall. soft-fall laughter of angels and the half-dozen inhabitants of good souls, all reclining in the crumbled foundations of our near-conquests. but the buildings of Heaven trickled down slowly— nothing but gold-laced cushion covers pumped full of helium. and we didn't mean to bring them down but we enjoyed piercing their tumbling walls with hairpins and andirons.

in the end, everyone had to go home; angels, neighborhood boys and sisters alike. conciliatory goodbyes as all sides left equals— no castles, only messes to clean before any parent returned home.

when there still were Octobers?

everyone dressed as the dead.

mothers dressed in black and white as movie starlets whose beauty died long before they had the consideration to do the same.

fathers dressed as the undead monsters they ~~could always be inspired to become when no one but family was watching~~ grew up terrified of in televisions, closets and adjacent bedrooms.

but we only had imagination enough to dress as literal deaths— decorating heads with bullet holes, stomachs of artificial entrails leaked from knife wounds, chests clenched in cardiac arrested movement. and we would lie like that— shallow breaths and eyes closed —all night long as neighborhood parents traveled from door to door to see those reenactments and to throw candy at those tiny bodies, trying to get them to move.

but we never did.

gentle snores eventually gave us away. then we were buried beneath blankets and quietly whispered:

– *Good night...*

's that sounded much like prayers.

waking the next morning to wash-off our someday situation; firmly instilling the belief we would find a way to effortlessly out-maneuver Death simply by waking.

she dressed as a long-forgotten sister.

arc-welding holes into the base of an unused garbage dumpster, post-toddler legs walking its wheels around town. only stopping when the brave dared a lid-lifted view. each giving an exaggerated:

– *Awww...*

at the creative costume as she never broke character— impaled in the sea of department store coat hangers.

570ˣ

it was the last year Christmas trees were around.

everyone since subjected to those gaudy plastic remembrances of what was.

this was what was.

for others, an icon conforming to the limitations of home. we simply leaned it where a wall should have been: a ten foot fir peaking over our ramshackle roof; a pinnacle of thousands of lights without one repetition; back then, we had more colors.

what we didn't have were walls to hold in the smell.

there remains a remnant of it in those chemical bottled scents some brew in potpourri pots to remind everyone of things passed— yet it does not compare. and neighbors all had confined trees, surely, but stepping outside they smelled the tree we erected stronger than what their homes held.

and its branches held the weight of ornamental old stories: the annunciation; the manger and its guests; the immaculate manger cesarean. all topped by a star so bright it brought travelers to it on holiday eve.

even before knowing it would be the last tree we would house, it felt like something special.

until the day after— just another dying thing among so many, impossible to believe it was ever any different.

Hell is the sound of siblings fighting.

and we brought Hell to wherever we were.

the desire to see one's own blood flow out of another—Cain's curiosity lingering in the language of our veins. we lived for the screams of the other. hearts beating while beaten or beating; preparing for the world to be fed by another unoriginal sin.

the mediator of slammed doors breaking it up when weapons became unequal: fists trumped by plastic dolls swung by their hair trumped by an empty bottle of watered down white wine trumped by a knife; never another weapon to trump it— always ending with a knife and a barricaded door. never willing to go around as the illusion of walls made us both feel safe.

lasting as long as we were left alone.

always reconciling at the heard footsteps of an approaching parent.

the cul-de-sac led to a faulty foundation.

cinderblocks crumbled like limestone with wrought iron pikes erected around edges of an unconstructed house. the post-school day remnants of the kingdom we conquered— we had a generation, too. we wanted its war to be justification: a search for meaning in the things we did.

so we impaled a thousand dolls on pikes: Barbies and thrift-story Barbie knock-offs; Cabbage Patch Kids with their cotton entrails blowing away in the wind; those creepy life-like plastic things that wet the bed when fed water and closed their eyes when reclined— never to open again as rust stains ran red down their bodies.

we were alive. justification enough to litter the world with carcasses of the never-were and no-longer-are living.

in the recessed ground within Gilgameshian walls we dug holes and covered them with old twigs; we tied taut trip-lines near those pikes; we constructed quicksand traps at every entrance with five-gallon buckets and the sand from neighborhood horseshoe pits. we were ready to kill to be the only ones living.

we only trapped ourselves.

the quicksand engulfed Andy, found eight days later by neighborhood dogs kind enough to excavate the body; then fought over until a few dozen chew-toy-size pieces were discovered in everyone's back yards.

the twig-covered holes rolled the ankles of those who knew to watch for them; even broke William's leg.

the trip lines were poorly hidden— only invisible at night, piece of mind knowing no one could come and take joy from the faulty foundation while we slept. tangling the feet of a neighborhood high school boy and his sweetheart sneaking out to do coupling things in the night. we found them— after cereal, cartoons and bus stop walks —impaled like their precursors; the most creepy perimeter dolls.

we brazenly played around them until summer came and their distended bodies ruined our world with unpleasant smells.

she volunteered dolls for the slaughter.

the last generation grew up never seeing a true toddler so their plasticked likenesses were disturbing: large eyes on larger heads, exoskeleton frames, genitalialess.

and all that was alienatingly forgivable.

factory-formed lips led to their deaths. constantly curled in almost-smiles— as though they were beings of perpetual happiness. she saw it all clearly: each generation giving near all of its happiness away to the next for them to do the same. again and again, down to the last.

she watched each punctured pop release names and endearments they held, knowing she was born in their image with nothing left to give.

5.15

hands were intertwined with Kendra Skiles'.

spinning in circles on the playground grass that crackled beneath twirling feet in a language of soon-to-be death no one listened to; she made impossible things— like the touch of a girl —feel possible. they were just playground games, sure, but if we could gain one girl's touch, why couldn't we have them all?

4.17

she knew she was filler.

one that would always be commented about by mothers with an aside of:

– *Oh, she's such a pretty girl.*

never a hope for being what everyone wanted for life; only for a day. not something that depresses a nine-year-old— an age that knows every day is a day and, in that, most want little more than to be spinning in the brittle grass with her. if their eyes wander? let it be; everyone knows— even if they leave town in search of something more —these boys could do no better than her.

5.13

father quit the mill to harvest land.

the temper thrown around ~~when we were thrown around at home~~ did not meet an acquiescent audience at the mill; always promising never to repeat unremembered actions.

the first time we had come home feeling important— after holding Kendra's hand for most of recess —father left work a bit more broken by unloved labor than ever before, taking the town's one road past father's family home and saw Don's still-growing garden before the next shift's whistle sounds.

at home, father filled the truck with few belongings.

then left.

we were home at the time so we went along; not knowing what else to do.

mother only said:

– *It's cruel to uproot children and move them to new places.* in the entire two-hour drive into the desert— said without pity or judgment: a simple fact observed while becoming a cruel truth.

asphalt gave way to gravel and gravel deteriorated to two eroded lines of dirt surrounded by grasshopper infested weeds singing a:

– *Welcome home!*

tune. when it ended, it ended at the door of an askew single-wide mobile home that wasn't mobile enough to get to any place better; no walls replaced by tin with less authority.

that first night father set to work, planting staple crops near— tomatoes and green beans, of course, but corn and wheat and potatoes and transparent bottles of Old No. 7 — as sand was planted in the acreage furthest away.

orderly rows of lumped dirt.

it was in a box brought along.

albums of photos taken to document the progression of mother and father; we found them tucked away with that strange object— running the three-meter length of the new home, holding it aloft and screaming in unison:

– *Mother, look! Mother, look! Mother, look!*
and mother looked and nodded in the near-shrug dismissive way mothers can nod. adding:

– *Another obsolete machine. They don't even make film for those things anymore. Put it back where you found it.*

mother would say we disobeyed; we considered it stalling for answers— asking obvious questions of what such a shiny thing could possibly be used for. of course, mother fell to our demanding curiosity for the sake of silence; calling it a camera.

we— again —asked the obvious.

and mother obviously answered:

– *What is worth documenting today?*
then mother found desired silence adorned with the wind-wind-wind-click. we posed for each other in ways we felt were important— imagining we were memorable. the photographer then drew stick-figure replicas of those poses to glue into a set of encyclopedias left by the trailer's last occupants. what could be more important?

and we felt worth documenting— until we sat down to appreciate makeshift albums. it was instantly obvious: the drawings were indistinguishable.

even when playing at being memorable, we were not.

we were allowed delusion for a day.

the one time we thought we would make it in this world.

first day at a new school, there was a moment when recess skimmed wallball balls flew perfectly by the school's best player and tethered others flew over the heads of its tallest.

a time when we were remembered by teachers who directed correct names and compliments toward the smiles we somehow manufactured with ease.

a time when we were named in whispers by popular girls in circles of giddy giggles.

it came with the mantle of:

– *New Kid.*

and we lived eight hours believing the hands of Kendra Skiles lifted us to another level.

in this new school there were new girls that made breathing difficult and— in that and them —we were happy to be breathing at all. dozens of girls populated the popular elite but it was obvious from a glance that Cameo Dowell demanded the most attention.

and we earned some in return... that first day.

then we came home.

walked from bus stop thru weeds where future money was supposed to grow, climbed into the new almost-home and smelled the poverty that had not had a chance to settle into clothes— might not happen that night or week, but it would happen. then there would be no hope for the hopes we had.

she could hold people like a sneeze.

like everyone in the world stopped to watch; all wanting to be the first to acknowledge the action with a:

– *Bless you.*

like it could be painful if released too soon or held too long.

– *Bless you.*

like it was something natural and forced all at once.

– *Bless you.*

like it was something, of course, blessed.

– *Bless you.*

like an irritation soon-to-be satiated.

– *Bless you.*

5.8

we experimented with skin color.

crayons held to matches to contour colors to bodies; salmon, cornflower, ultra yellow, bittersweet, prussian blue. blistered flesh held together with wax— attempting to be more beautiful than before.

or— after inhaling them deeply; believing changes could be as permanent as labels claimed —we marked ourselves with markers. one arm opaque, another slapdashed with the dexterity of an off-hand's attempt— gaps in the ever-present lack of color.

but it left.

slowly.

fading the person we never liked back into being.

4.4

they stopped teaching what had been taught.

reading, writing and arithmetic were for a world that was going somewhere; no one believed that any longer— obedience is what would sustain society. so we were taught to be obedient; not in the way father was taught but in the way dogs were taught: some beaten, some rewarded. we were beaten with:

– *Sit. Stay.*

commands; allowed to do little more than draw dreams of the world we wanted to live in. and, just like a dog never taught the command:

– *Come.*

we lost track of if ever we were wanted.

we were still institutionally taught to cover hearts.

either with hands or hats or words— starting every school day with petite right hands held as protection; watched over by teachers who stood as iconic lonely guardians.

that same third grade year we witnessed the school's first objection to the act: a meek new student unable to hold the visage of grandeur for a day, speaking thru a legible letter from home citing a nontheistic belief in the need to love. all it took was the wry proclamation:

– *Well, it looks like Leroy will be abstaining...*

by Ms. Danford, leaving reasons unknown and that unknown word— abstain —undefined. it was all we needed, tormenting the new kid with his new name: A. Stain. something so catchy it made the unfortunate birth name go unnoticed.

but, as mean as we were, it was an important lesson learned.

we learned telling him all recess how everyone knew his underpants were stained would make him lock himself in the bathroom until the letter writing mother arrived.

we learned spilled ink on his homework would keep him after class explaining what was already known, tears staining Ms. Hatch's desk in ignored pleas for more than understanding.

we learned it took less than a year of this cruelty for A. Stain to return home from school to drink every beneath-the-sink hidden bottle stickered with those neon green frowny faces.

we learned what became of an unguarded heart.

she exhibited cruelty as a seduction.

from those threadbare cutoff jean shorts with tie-dye leggings beneath to the big hair dominating an overly attractive head, everything cried she was from or destined for big city somewhere; never acknowledging any little someone from any little podunk town she would never be forced to set foot in— already meticulous at nine.

so none of it— neither cruelty nor seduction —could have been accidental.

she stopped attempts to talk to her before they began with a practiced glare of contempt. leaving the would-be speaker thinking:

– *Yes, what I would have said was stupid anyway...*
and, shortly after:

– *How could such a pretty face be so terrifying for an instant?*

it was probably that latter thought that kept so many coming back, opening their mouths as if to say something— experiments in the impermeability of beauty. and she always obliged the same look, knowing there was nothing attractive or anything to be gained in progressive niceties.

5.14

maybe the hamsters asked for it.

after only three weeks living with us, we liked them no more than their claws and puncturing teeth liked our flesh. maybe the amply provided pellets and water suckled from a far too convenient metal nub were not what they wanted— maybe they, too, wanted air conditioning and a sense of adventure.

hamsters are curious creatures.

and the fall crops were harvested. the planted ground had grown into new land, sold to people who needed it to build things better than what we had. father would have been content kicking the dirt with newfound faraway neighbors, echoing the things said:

– *Not as good as the year before.*

– *Nope. Worst take since...*

as we avoided their stares.

father would have been happy to stay but mother wanted a vacation.

maybe the hamsters wanted one too. maybe that's why mother put them in a paper bag then safely secured it in the freezer.

vacations were a week long.

always to the west— father threatening every fifteen minutes to pull the car over and beat us until quiet; stopping the car every hour ~~to make good on threats~~ in search of rest stop bathrooms.

when we finally got there we witnessed what the sea washed on shore: mammals, fish, crustaceans. it proved that the land was not the only thing to reject the things it held. beachfront motels adapted by selling miniature barbecues and cleavers; a thousand mile buffet to hack away at. seaweed always available for sushi rolls while alternated cauldrons were filled with rice or boiling water every thirty yards.

and those incessant preschool fishing poles littered about as props— putting the line into the mouths of a whale or shark, holding the reel as a prop as cartoonists illustrated cartoons of themselves being anywhere else doing real art.

it led to empty arcades. no one played skeeball or tried to claw stuffed animals into existence or pilfered tickets for saltwater taffy and cracked gimcracks. we poked aquatic eyes to feel the film and see how far they'd squish before becoming almost solid. we rode near-dead manatees flopping in circles; we stacked shellfish in parapets and walls and lobbed jellyfish over the similarly built barricades manned by similar children.

we returned to hotel rooms sunburned, stung, bloodied from the exploding shelled shrapnel of our own fortifications— refusing father's obsession with swimming pool swimming —in complete agreement with the sea for refusing to house such combative refuse.

mother couldn't have meant to murder the hamsters.

we believed her to be above the maliciousness of beautiful girls while simultaneously believing her to be the most beautiful woman in the world. we were naive like that.

had mother meant to kill the hamsters she would have chosen something more robust than a paper bag. as it was, they simply shredded their confines, cuddled for warmth, feasted on frozen vegetables and reproduced— there was little else to do in the eternal darkness. and then their offspring came, suckling for warmth and taught a creole braille of freezer bag indentations and scratches in the ice to cave-scrawl their glass wall ancestry and the ever-present ammonia smells of tainted wood shavings.

still, if mother had meant to murder the hamsters— it worked.

returning home, we forced the centuries of hamster civilization from its triumph of icebox culture back into glass boxes where shavings couldn't be ice sculpted into commemorative wonders of miniature worlds. their malaise gave way to genocide, cannibalism and eventual suicide by the few survivors.

whichever was meant, we learned to fear mother's terrifying efficiency.

father sat anxious all winter.

mother sat anxious with him— ~~needing someone to scream at so~~ no one was allowed to leave the house; father's mind riddled with the fears of what other men could provide. never wanting to circle bar parking lots. not that mother was the one to seek refuge in another when times were hard but it didn't stop father's ~~violent~~ fears.

this was the winter They decided calendars became obsolete— stopping where the last calendar ended; perpetually living December 32nd. it solved the problem of birthdays: never holding celebrations for births impossible to celebrate.

so, being told seasons might not ever arise again, father watched for breaks in the gray sky for any sign of something to make life from. eventually the wait was abandoned and father worked the frozen ground like it was a 13-year-old whore; knowing its most profitable years would soon be over. forsaking more of the staple crops, planted dirt littered more of the acreage than the year before.

land was the cash crop.

each grain planted— if well fertilized and watered daily —could grow the land eight to ten inches. seven acres could easily become forty if the ground gave another good year. all sold off to mother's brother's construction firm who erects subdivisions of identical houses in seven days— maybe not as benign a trait as once thought.

we held sad eyes aloft to elders.

a survival look learned; little energy needed to be kept sad— a backhand and a discouraging comment then we were left alone with fantastical thoughts defying eyes. those never learning that look— always holding laughter in the space between eyebrows and cheek bones —demanded the attention of those put here to put others in their place.

we watched peers with smiling eyes pulled from class to be caned, raped and have old wounds salted. always returning to homeroom seats with tears in those smiling eyes— but they still smiled. for obvious reasons.

no matter the meanness they forced upon the young, they could not rescind the things we did to this world.

we would have preferred the place they remembered but— if we did make this world a Hell —some of us smiled with eyes knowing there were never more deserving people to be punished.

4.13

she never figured out how to fix glances.

always inquisitive with brows bent downward like a cartooned villain. always questioning the:

– Why?

's of this world everyone unwillingly accepted as-is.

one of them killed her; either eyes or They— one day disappearing from a:

– Wish you were here!

terrified classroom. each remaining child left to imagine how it got out of hand; how— with each beating she took —eyes would ask:

– Why are you doing this?

a repeated question answered with repeated violence.

that's how most saw it happening.

but she saw it firsthand. each striking hand taking tears freely given. tasting them as Their own eyes questioned why they tasted so good. striking again and again and she never gave the satisfaction of an answer, either.

the irrigation pipes did not move themselves.

so we walked— nail in pocket; twice a day —thru the progressively barren field.

main valve screwed down, hauled to the next head then screwed up. each pipe lifted overhead to drain while walking toward center until balanced— then tight-rope taken twenty yards and added to the head. repeated until there was neither more pipe nor field; repeated in a tedium only grade schoolers can know in the hurry to get it done before catching the morning bus and again after school.

but it was almost worth it when the valve was released and the sprinkler heads all clogged with the things pump-sucked from the irrigation ditch: tadpoles, minnows and— once —a mammal of some sort, probably a mouse. we walked those lines with a viciously raised nail to scramble caught things into enough pieces to allow the water to fill the field.

a welcome situation of permitted violence bookending civil affronts suffered at school.

we sketched the things we thought we were meant to build.

family traits emerging without consent.

strictly forbidden by mother to construct anything, drawings lay hidden in the holes in walls father ~~punched~~ made— like we hid when they were made; vacuous monuments of fearful moments holding these new hopes.

the blueprints of a new world were worked on nightly in the only hours we had to ourselves— moonlit sills embossing pages with wood grain. we were determined— in the few minutes of free time we gave it thought —to glue together this world we broke.

we survived two more years by doodling doodles of better places.

and by watching Cameo Dowell.

favored by fortune when the shifting of each grade found she was in the same classroom. we had a never-could-be-popular last name that kept enough alphabetically assigned seats between that omnipresent gaze so she rarely caught it. even then— after so long living with it —even she tired of throwing glares in response.

but eventually we were taken to the middle school where we unfortunately fit in and no one attractive was allowed; watching grade school doors barred shut as we were ushered to the place for children who would learn to be invisible people.

hallways were swept one last time and teachers straightened desks in the final illustration of order they could ever hope to impose on others.

we left and no others lingered behind in need of being taught nonsense and falsehoods— the elementary school sat in ordered vacancy; one more reminder of what would no longer be.

still, in that new place, girls had such new features we believed them to be women. most weren't quite curves. simple transitions: contusions. and, while being fascinated, we could not find beauty in those bodies.

of course there was Tiffany Drake, fully matured and then some, that we watched run in gym class. fascinated. but never watching with the reverence of belief given to a smile. or a holding of hands. or an aura of dominance that makes those in its presence feel this failed world will be okay.

she was desired without being desirable.

so— at times when words should have been shared— she received in response what she deserved: silence. in it could be read a kind of reverence— an acquiescence to whatever quality she might have had worth revering.

but it generally happened over a phone blaring the electronic drone speakers make to simulate the silence each side was abandoned to. not to be malicious or reverential. she simply had nothing to say and the boys were entertained by themselves with muffled moans and exhalations they weren't secure enough to share. when they finished, there was not the niceties of:

    – You hang up first.
    – No, you hang up first...
    – No, you hang up first...
    – No, you...

simply a:

    – See you at school.

as she was left looking for some other voice to make uncomfortable nights bearable.

the radio, surely, had someone talking— stating some wrong done because the speaker would not get away with doing it and would want someone to speak out if such a thing were done to him. and somewhere was forgotten family in a time zone where they would have been awake at hours not so odd; telling stories of familiar names doing things unfamiliar enough to make them worth telling.

but all were one-sided stories; she was not needed for them to happen or for the retelling of them. some stories are more isolating than silence where participation is required from all sides.

but she is not desirable; something already known. the reason why the dial tone is listened to until it gives way to disconnected pulses desiring she not set the receiver down and end their existence.

the slowness with which it all died felt normal.

a few things refusing to rise with each rotation. not entire crops; some seeds simply stayed seeds— possibly contented by their potential to be something more so they never tried to become it.

possibly.

but the things that did grow were harder to keep alive; the grass seemed greenish but was no longer hospitable to bare feet. underneath the living was the prickly dead. and the ground did not grow from the ground like it did years before.

still, there was enough money coming in to haul in other mobile homes and weld them onto the immobile one. new-found independence offered in the distances kept from others— no longer forced to share rooms or meals or conversations. we had the luxury of becoming strangers to those always forcing the ideals of contentious love.

and in newfound isolation, we began to execute the long drawn plans— finally finalized.

first: a rock was buried in the expansive back yard— watered three times a day —until we were able to uproot it from the exhausted ground: a miniature planet lifted and set in motion.

second: we built new creatures out of clipped chicken wire and blood. but not people. we knew worlds were not made better by people and cats and deers and cows and goats and all the other animals made by the unimaginative god of this world. we were aiming to make people with hippo feet and pterodactyl wings and clawed hands and triceratops horns and kitten ears because girls liked kittens— but the material was too small for such detail. they mostly came out looking like upright ants. still, we loved them as creators should love their creations. breathing existence into each one; watching the dozen staggering in the confusion instilled by burdensome life.

third: we left them to populate their second-chance world.

even in the early years we lost peers to childish games.

back when misguided efforts of recycling and other forms of conservation promised the possibility of generations being able to live off of others' refuse if scientists ever found a way to make another generation.

certainly not as many as were lost in later days but class size dwindled by three in seventh grade. the first— Chad Brewer —a victim to a good throw of a bad batch of synthetic food supplements in a fatal food fight. the second— Chad Peck —was ruled autoerotic asphyxiation. and then there was one of the many nameless girls of little beauty— not even finding a name then, just another empty seat with a feeling it was not always empty.

but they were all recycled: hair intertwined to resemble cobwebs so people could place them in the corners of houses to remove after someone noticed; fingernails were planted in dirt and watched to see if they would grow beyond the grave as almost plants; flesh fed to students poor enough to be on the school meal plan; bones burned brittle and used as classroom chalk.

and that chalk— when held on its side and pulled across the green board —screamed screeching screams from the afterlife. incomprehensible— terrifying enough to know they were no place happy but hard to tell if it was anyplace worse.

she had a name.

interestingly obscure but pronounceable— said at home with inflected love she never had the chance to hear elsewhere. in a better world— maybe the one grandparents drained and left to rot —she would have heard it a few times in high school; junior year when that body finally grew into itself.

after so long without that spoken word of love pronounced as her name, she would have reciprocated— finding love in its reflection.

some happinesses are solidly built in symmetry. in a better world— maybe the one that will be here when this one is gone —she would have found this in some nameless man whose only joy was saying hers.

yes, in that better world, she would have been worshiped in each greeting.

here, she died nameless where games of love are rarely played with lower stakes.

somewhen, the sky grew.

long ago. we never knew it any way but the way it is now. but in that newfound space, clouds found the freedom to do whatever they wished: morph, rain, dissipate to nothingness, cover the night sky so no one could make wishes of their own.

carcasses of old trees were still around— fallen —holding down the ground; their toppled girth almost as tall as the still-rooted gnarled twigs we were accustomed to calling trees— unworthy descendants. the sky was an attainable goal in parents' time: the largest of the green monstrosities scraping it, a limb-ladder conduit to something bigger.

but maybe they weren't scraping the sky at all.

maybe they apical-meristem-hooked the blue to tether the endless within reach.

maybe they are heroes; one great push-off collapsing the trunks of the ancients to keep the heavens from falling onto this world.

or maybe we fell them all; each sawed collision quaking the ground lower and lower beneath our only conception of the third dimension.

whichever, the sky leaving us or the ground failing us again by falling, the endless of the blue became out of reach. the second-coming of trees of our childhood— tiny shoots —shot up from the roots of the fallen with amazing grace. ambitious. easily a foot in the first week, six inches the second, then an inch in six months; discouraged by distance.

they led by example and died out quickly. but we remembered the example set and grew in spurts the same way; outgrowing middle school desks overnight.

we grew long after our landscape abandoned its attempts.

we grew in spurts that belittled our parents. a head— a head-and-a-half —taller than them because we knew we could be more massive than anything in this world.

the skeletons of dead wood curled and bowed to us, timidly growing back toward the ground. in the freedom of newfound space that mother and father never had, we structured ourselves with a stature that would stagger any god we could think of; our fault for not being more imaginative— our greatest obstacle among so many.

she did not stop growing when other girls did.

an irreversible mistake; not paying attention to the norm— even the boys knew not to push it quite so far. slouches and dropped shoulders tried to hide height but could only do so much...

she watched as the few boys near her mistaken height took the tiniest of girls to the school dances; totemic boys building miniatures around them to appear as men. and she tried to find humor in it all as parents offered near-incestuous praise of:

– *The boys just don't know what they're missing, honey.* but the beauty she possessed was outlying the norm; deranged in its brazen obviousness.

5.17

the few remaining recess sports were waged on blacktop.

new superstitions killed the old. no more fear of sidewalk cracks; now the plagued ground was toed to— only fearing we would lose our own lives if it was touched.

wallball exchanged for dodgeball; tetherball for full-contact basketball— hopscotch for cigarettes, slutty looks and clawed eyes or hair lost in manicured fists. these were the violent alterations we believed we discovered on our own.

and maybe they were ours.

taught to peers by peers.

able to deny the influences suffered elsewhere by the megalomaniacal fancy that we instigated all of it.

4.6

when we were given a war it was labeled: cold.

a fight to the death without weapons— a generational skirmish where we were chronologically favored. both old and young saw the other as cruel— callous —for either bringing them into it or for ruining what once was...

an infertile world's very last:

– *Chicken or the egg?*

problem.

we only picked sides because mother and father entrenched themselves into theirs so long ago. but we did not see them as evil for bringing life into a lifeless world; not even accusing them of the sin of being ill-informed— only lacking clairvoyance. an unreasonable thing to expect, but wars are rarely waged on reason.

so we half-heartedly yelled at parents and lived in cold war nuclear homes hellbent on fission.

before school we spray-painted mantras on concrete surfaces in the practiced penmanship of an illiterate generation's scrawl:

– *ULL DIE! UR UNFIT 4 R WORLD!*

exhilarated and simultaneously saddened by the possibility we may be fit for such a place.

father's parents died in the time of our war.

    its first casualties, actually. found in the confines of their tiny bedroom— victims of carried-away youth with cold fists proclaiming their time was here. father's mother fallen across the vanity; father's father alone in the marital bed. unrecognizable. not due to the violent nature of Death but because both bodies reclaimed their long-lost aspects of youth.

    tones set in life were lost as simple as that.

    the vanity's mirror framed a scene where it was easy to believe these aspects of lost people had— for a moment before departure —found a way to love each other again.

4.1

horoscopes became simplified.

broken into two categories: those born pre-we and everyone else.

the morning paper told the former category their lucky numbers, prescription drug concoctions to make a mind believe it was living twenty years earlier, drug chasing cocktails to make them work faster and some sort of benign inspirational message— something like:

– *You'll be dead soon. Hang in there.*

while we were given a blurb above the obituaries, always reading:

– *Today, these are your fault.*

and we read them— from Adams to Young —wondering who was at fault in earlier days— probably cancers. but we learned quickly what few other generations ever did: dying is the only expectation everyone lives up to.

4.18

eighth grade ended.

we watched doors boarded shut without any cleaning or preparation; optimism, at that point, that there would be no more coming. and then— after the first five days oogling junior and senior girls —we found the first weekend of our generation.

they could not keep them hidden forever.

found an earned Saturday in an overslept haze; walking into a world where things obviously once felt possible— and, for a moment, we forgot the impossibility of the possible and believed we were capable of it.

beckoned by a baseball dugout; an everyday fallout shelter of concrete seemingly more alive buried than the dead grass above. and within it was Casey Snyder— a sophomore designated to be everyone's first girlfriend. we took our places in line and waited.

sometime Sunday— just before twilight when her face became little more than the feel of warm flesh where we were reflected in silhouettes of lit eyes —we had our shot: thirty seconds of small talk and two minutes making out. that was it. knowing the turn was over by the silence that ensued.

she learned to be suspicious of well-rehearsed words.
beginning to blend together with:
– *You have beautiful eyes...*
and inevitably ending as:
– *I love you.*
in monotone.
but suspicion is not an action in and of itself— letting each boy practice practically enjoyable things, waiting to deny the final thing they wanted with so many wasted words.

5.14

mother's parents came for the memory of a holiday.

a lingering Fall sentiment from a time when people were thankful for lives.

first contact with that side of the family. the few traits that lingered in the bloodline were seen beneath aged features withered on broken bodies: mother's father's bridged back broken by a lifetime of unreasonable demands; mother's mother's beauty betrayed by everything in the world but individual hope.

most importantly: we saw a oncewas aptitude for life we were deprived of— observing eugenic origins that could have done anything. and we witnessed this without resentment. in fact, we never felt as blessed as we did when we compared ourselves to them because even these people— endowed with the weapons to make it in the world —failed to come away from it unscathed.

we were forever immune to that particular disappointment.

so we listened to their stories of persecution in good days to make us feel better about these not-so-good days. not that we would have wanted to attend their time; nothing in those stories were made better by being there. if all that we would oneday be were hunkered bodies and stories, then we decided then and there to live lives worth talking about.

and maybe we talked too much to these ancestral strangers, pulling mother's father aside to say:

– *We are alike. Come see!*

pulling large hands— so long clenched that they could no longer close —across the expansive backyard to the peopled rock rotating there. and mother's father long watched the thousands of ant-like people in pursuit of people-like things.

they killed and copulated and accrued things unneeded.

but they also built bridges.

mother's father nodded and we returned to the confines of a graceless dinner, saying only:

– *It might be what you were built for...—*

we watered the grass after its death.
   giving it a golden sheen instead of letting it remain a
brittle brown that broke beneath shoes.

father once dreamed of child sport stars—

but all anyone watched was girls volleyball so it was the only sport the school kept; the only one that turned a profit. ten dollars for general admission, fifty for a private booth.

so we inadvertently alarm-clock-slaughtered another dream of father's.

all settling on a family of sport goers— near-fanatics — witnessing those too-short shorts scissoring in pursuit of the ball. short enough that we believed we were aficionados on female anatomy... until Natasha Holloway.

we entered indiscriminate movie houses to find darkness in the day; sitting in the back and exploring the contours young bodies made in ill-fitting clothes. fingering front-clasped bras like an inexperienced thief hearing sirens. hands in back pockets to feel the thrill of safely invading clothing. to this day, there is not another's dental line better known— memorized with the zeal of early relationships, lips leaving contact just long enough to the air with:

– *I love you...*

expected lies.

she saw salvation in men.

learned from a mother who found it in a man— or in the few men who came with a few marriages at various times when salvation was needed.

as such, she heard her mother proclaim tongue-in-cheek:

– *Hallelujah!*

testimonies with a sinner's conviction whenever a new boy was brought home. mothers are never imaginative enough to wish daughters better circumstances than they were born with. both witnessing the default virtue of youth in each new boy that her mother insisted she take inside her.

but virtues are— at times —hard to insistently take from the inadvertently virtuous. and panic set in with each fearful refusal of things unknown. she was taught no other way to keep anyone interested— if there ever was another way.

a quickly learned fact:

girls who see boys with a girl believe them worthy of attention. it, in turn, makes misguided boys believe they could be worthy of the attention of better girls.

so we watched and wondered what kind of men we could be with each one. we felt larger around Rachel Wright— even with her wide eyes at eye level —shoulders feeling they were expansive enough to carry anything in comparison to her tiny frame.

we felt stable around Laurén Fadel— loudly announcing we did not receive the brunt of what this insane world could distribute.

so we left one girl to find out who we would be with others. leaving the way we were left before: in silence. responded to inversely with late night crying calls demanding answers to the same demanded question that went unanswered— impossible to tell someone better than we were that we were too good for them.

still, every girl touched was a reminder of the ones who weren't or, worse, the ones we couldn't. all those attractive girls who gave themselves also gave rise to constant reminders of the beautiful— Shannon Bex, Blair Hanson, Effie Bisch —who never would.

so we rapidly went thru the ones we could get; playing possum— feeling dead —with those who tried so hard to make us feel alive.

she was a series of contradictory girls.

1 – she wore her body draped over shoulders. yes, loose fitting. but not in a way others found unappealing— its laxness fit in its own way. simply a natural burden of flesh grounding what was trying to transcend this place.

2 – she forced cigarette smoke to linger everywhere she went, leaving many to comment on the disgusting habit and how it tainted her appearance. only the privileged few were given a taste of lip gloss to let senses mix; an amalgamation of contradictory sensations fighting for olfactory recognition.

3 – she felt waking to herself was punishment so nights were spent on the phone, falling asleep with it near— hoping whomever wouldn't hang up before morn.

4 – she was, at times, a profane display of beauty.

5 – she straight-face sold sincere lies.

she would cease being one when interest waned, moving on to being the next; never looking too different and always experimenting with the next intolerable action that postured contradictions could force someone to love.

magic words became outdated.

even the most well-known ones. rabbits no longer hid in the linings of hats, doors were at the whim of metal trinkets instead of syllables— even that one engrained since birth, reminded in that threatening tone of:

– *What do you say?*

they only held the power to inspire laughter when used.

so we tucked away:

– *Abracadabra.*

– *Open sesame.*

– *Please.*

and spoke like the others. not as incessantly, no. only so far as to adopt their few words in public— standing in lines for synthetic food, telling the cashier:

– *Give me a...*

– *I'll have a...*

then a number. always numbers: the clinical usurpation of order in randomness. sixteen could buy anything; thirteen identified any book; twelve operated in the stead of a name; ten could touch-tone sing their way to find the voice of someone worlds away...

lawless numbers. none with the privilege of vowels or forcing one to follow another in queue like QU— none allowed the obscure mystery of Z or X; all used, more or less, evenly. a democratic death to one more magical thing.

4.14

she practiced old incantations.

each discovered in library books— back cover pulled from slips —copying check-out names of the deceased onto an exposed arm. razor-written down wrists in hopes of knowing the world they found. each word a color theory relearned— red added to time fades to black-stitched emergencies and eventual purpled flesh ridges.

she practiced down each arm in failed magics calling to be taken anywhere else.

62¹⁰
(shoo.)

mother and father left for the funerals.

mother's mother and mother's father were finally caught by one great uncle's trap or another. left behind, we were never told one of those:

– *In case of an emergency, there are instructions in the jewelry box in my bathroom...*

but we were nosy children. and mother was a superstitious woman incapable of saying the words:

– *In case of an emergency...*

so we eventually found the Etch-A-Sketch death note in the jewelry box.

no, that's not right.

or— if it is —it is misleading: it never housed jewelry.

the lifted lid revealed the silver screen with red edges sitting on rounded, cushioned indentations where rings were meant to be pressed and displayed with their best faces forward; but mother wore the only ring she owned. scattered between those vacant cushions and the gently laid Etch-A-Sketch death note were three liberty dollars with numbers inscribed on them coinciding with mother's marriage and our birth-years.

all the same, that deathnote— every word connected by a jagged line —was the first thing we always read every time we were left alone. all the reflective words mother could never bring herself to say. shaken anew for each new departure but they were always similar— each in her cursive knobbed writing with the ghost of the last letter lingering —and they always started the same:

– *If/you're– reading/this,/I'm– dead—*

so that every time mother left we felt left behind; re-imagining a dozen different deaths. terrified until they returned.

then we only felt lied to— betrayed by their survival.

she gave it up.

    one action destroying an old hope; even if there were still unicorns around, she would no longer be able to see them.

5.19

we learned to fold into hugs.

common greeting of the sexes exploited.

instead of compressing bodies to feel folds and contours, we learned to create a negative of their shape with a slouch, a turn of the head, a torso twist so we were only separated by fabric touching. a contortion memorized to mimic later— filling the empty space with plaster, constructing Pygmalion near-likenesses to commemorate the bodies they would someday destroy. all lining the dirt driveway; colonnades of sketches not quite worthy of marbled goddess homages.

4.14

the plaster promenade had its flaws.

the weather took an interest in the first one; she was rain etched and colored to its liking, smoothing out the fingerprints that constructed the visage— withering sharp edges away until she was as diminutive as desired.

the fourth one looked as tho she was compiled while contaminated with the pox. she was formed with an impurity; maybe sand got into the mix. maybe she did not want to be composed of those certain plaster pieces. or maybe it was a braille spelling out love notes, a memoir or a plea to be Galatea.

the last one toppled; top heavy beyond the model she was modeled after— an attempt to improve upon what shouldn't have been touched.

the rest left in their own time: following the lead of this world that trickled to pieces. still, most lasted longer than the beauty they were meant to immortalize.

5.2

there was still hot water.

a constant in all recently lived lives; everyone feeling relieved beneath screaming streams of steam.

it provided a universality of moments— everything between waking and walking out the front door — nothing anyone could do in that time was new. and the same day relived was too new to destroy those contented somnambulist moments lived by everyone in time; lasting as long as the warmth of water could be held within bones. even when the television told its tales over raised cups of chemicals of another day edging everyone closer to the end of the world, it didn't matter— it was artificial warmth, easily stolen. sure. but it was a feeling of warmth all the same.

and we possessed it.

then a turned knob and the door's strength faded, forcing relinquishment of that simple contentment to what refused to be controlled. threshold standing in daily amazement— waiting for acclimation.

but it never came.

always wondering if everyone always felt that way, too.

we fell in love with the girl in a long blue coat.

three of four buttons buttoned to hold her in ways we instantly knew we wanted to— feeling, for the first and only time, complete at the site of her. granted: reddened hair and green eyes were a universal aesthetic. yes. but the high-bridged nose could have been an offense to anyone but a bridge-builder's kin; all atop a hidden body tucked inside that simple coat sheltering pieces we had never had to learn to live without.

sheer proximity fluttered stomach and caused a breathless chest to throb in vacuous need of her.

it was in that December 32nd summer of eleven weekends before junior year. we approached with an outstretched hand and an introduction of:

– *Once upon a time.*

knowing all good stories begin that way.

there were things smoked and giggles giggled somewhere along a stagnant stream where the last of the midnight frogs serenaded awkward kisses until we were caught between dawn and sunrise on the day she was to leave town.

words were said. not a one was:

– *After.*

or:

– *Happily.*

or:

– *Ever.*

tho, at first, it hardly mattered. we were not to be blamed if she did not feel what we felt— tho, we can be blamed for what we stole from her: the breathing done close together allowed pieces to escape and we felt we'd always feel more complete than ever.

she had endearing faults.

like listening to the same song— on repeat —for a week without ever learning the words to anything more than the chorus; then forgetting having ever liked the song so much but still having a nostalgic love for the band.

or she would argue points known to be wrong for the thrill of arguing them.

or she would allow the features of her face to conflict— a smile coupled with condemning eyes or a malicious smirk accompanying raised eyebrows of interest.

consequences of endearing faults were that daily letters received from once-upon-a-time boys went forgotten and she tumbled toward a man born between generations— someone with stories of The Better Time but likely to live until the end as well; a nostalgic 20-something knowledge-able on every subject. and she— honestly —loved this tran-sitory lover of broken-time girls who formulated the same formulaic attraction with scripted words.

so, when he left— as people are apt to do —she remem-bered only him and not the words she was attracted to which allowed other makeshift liturgists to fill the gaps she was left with.

mother never used benign endearments like:

  – Darlin'.

and/or:

  – Hon.

those words we needed then.

after unreciprocated love, desperation set in.

so we sought out those habitually used words in the all-night places where they flourished: diners and convenience stores. wrapped in blankets beneath gumshot tables or tucked to one side of the snack isle. and the:

  – Are you okay, hon?

and/or:

  – Darlin', do you need any help?

made the cigarette smoke and/or fluorescent lights possess a certain comfort— permitted belief that someone cared — before the police escort home.

4.2

she was named for a forgotten season.

high on imbibed spirits and ready to emulate the trajectory of oranged leaves— always excused in the act of emptying bottles by saying they will be someday molotovs. a revolution of weightless somedays.

and she recruited posthumous pets to the cold war by giving them new names: Freedom, Egalité, Bullet. never telling anyone if she had an army beneath ground ready to rise to the occasion or if it was just one very confused dead dog.

she compiled the instruments of war: knives, rope, gas masks, reliable lighters. waiting for the day when they would be useful anywhere but the bedrooms of boys hoping to die to ideals that offer bloodless deaths.

5.15

suicide class was mandatory.

we were too many and they were too few. so junior year started with a five minute sex education never mentioning HPV, herpes or crabs; divided by gender and told:

– *Do what you want. What does it matter now?*

then we were transferred to a small room with funneled light linking a clicking projector to a far wall— a moving image meant to show how sexy suicide can be. no introduction or faculty oversight; we sat ourselves and watched fidgety alabaster legs— cropped at the thigh in the upper left corner —fall from elegant black cloth onto bare feet, toes curled over the edges of the chair it all stood upon. minutes without movement did not matter; we would have watched those legs forever, not knowing how they could be improved— a temporary remedy for the girl in the blue coat.

then they stepped into the center of the frame. the dress needed time to catch up, which flashed her bare hip onscreen. slowed to give the appearance gravity had less of a hold on the beautiful; making the thrashing that happened when her feet never touched ground appear as a dance. and, watching, we were sure if it slowed further then the curves of hips would spell the names of everyone we would ever lust after— far more than the blue coat girl.

when it ended— when the film slapped itself against the machine invading the room with that profane light devoid of her —we looped it back together the best we knew how.

we got it backwards.

she thrashed in reverse that time, the example of life started still and fought to regain itself on the chair.

we would have watched it again— from step to death — but there was not enough time left to watch it in reverse afterward. so we sat in the dark, blinking as fast and loudly as any film projector— trying to rekindle any light-embossed portion of her.

come morning, eight suicides had already happened.
another eight left us that weekend.

they were the ones no one wanted to see go— the ones that had something intrinsic to offer: charisma, a good smile, undeveloped beauty resembling the precursor to perfection. these were the only ones confident enough to dance the steps of the woman in the black dress.

by Monday, the afterworld already claimed the best of the living.

those incantations eventually found a final silence.

the last thing scrawled down arms was the birth certificate liturgy she should have tried first; the only name that would never heal.

father gave driving lessons.

pointing to levers and switches and then the road— watching as we repeatedly stalled the automobile down dirt then onto the highway. father was getting old ~~so let inanimate objects act out violent acts of long ago~~; surely thinking we would be just as likely to die with or without his presence in the automobile.

and we felt freedom.

hellbent to travel over mountains to the land of the girl in the blue coat.

but we never got that far, returning wreckage home just before dusk.

a small inconvenience. new old cars were easy to find; people were dying everywhere without heirs. a few years before, estate sales sold off things cheaply— but money became more valuable than the things it could purchase: the last bits of paper scrawled with numeric literature comprehensible to all.

so we watched where buzzards circled.

beneath them were the near-dead— scents announcing the soon-to-happen; decay getting ahead of Death by a few days. the town walked with eyes to the skies. some houses had already been ransacked as the almost-living sat on the porch watching possessions passing on before them... tired of shooing away all buzzards.

we saw it in the driveway of an encircled farm house after leaving populative limits: a 280 SE Mercedes Benz. old man running to the porch to shotgun-wave us away but we knew he was out of shells— the too few buzzards writhing on the ground showed there was little to fear from his aim, anyway.

we met Uncle #4 on the failed family property.

it was the last hour of the backyard planet; those mini-lives brandishing mini-souls that cured war, cancer and unhappiness— all without the use of pills.

it was dusk—father kneeling in the field as mother prepared a soup of nutritional supplements —when we sneaked a final peak at the last living thing we knew. watching it drown as we managed a:

– *Hello, Great Uncle.*

while he shook, shivered and zipped.

there were expected sounds of dribbling; of popping bubbles of off-color foam; of mother's father's brother saying:

– *This isn't what you were meant to build, kid.*

then there was the unexpected silence: not a miniature scream to be heard as bodies streamed in the stutter-stop of fluid building and breaking thru grained dirt-dams between feet. thinking of no way to save any of it so only said:

– *Would you like to stay for dinner?*

mother made enough for everyone by not eating—watching the guest while worriedly wringing hands, twisting one over the other in the way some people are known to do over coffee.

neither mother nor father asked why mother's Uncle came just in case they were the answer.

we were meant to create something.

so we created backseat distractions from thoughts of a far away girl; fathering abortions in the only place owned. sharing those four wheels of forest green liberated wealth with whomever would allow such rebelliously lascivious acts to be committed with them.

honestly, the motions made were premature— barely enjoyable and only served to make composites of the automobile's inhabitants in miniature. but we read in ancient lore that this was the way to make love. another attempt at building something to repair this world.

and ultrasounds showed something made so we loudly proclaimed:

– Look at that heartbeat! Isn't that strong? That's what we made so it must be love! That one will shirk the trend, surely. We'll bring new life into this world.

but it was a joke with a timelined punchline; dangerous if taken too far.

everything— after all —had become barren. after six months it would simply die in there. shrivel. if left alone it would blue and mummify, clinging to womb walls— knowing it would never get so close to the living again.

but for five months we were parents.

and names picked were spray painted blue on clinic walls when we found out the gender— the same room serving as nursery and morgue when a shopvac with sharp dentures sucked him away. still, he held on long enough so we could say our greetings and goodbyes all at once. then the lifeless lump of flesh sailed away on a sea of holy water just in case he one-day decided to come back for revenge on the world that refused to nurture him.

but he never would.

that was when we knew: we were living beyond the pages of a book long ago written. The End was where we started— a meaningless symmetry forced into pages too pointless

to even be considered an epilogue. just those four blank sheets waiting for the cover to close.
   nothing could be made of our actions.

she scalded skin worn the night before.

burning away layers— sitting beneath shower faucets, thinking other-languagely thoughts of:

– *Le ciel est bleu.*

until there was nothing left of the person who made the mistakes almost remembered.

one day it was snowing, the next was 78°F—

seasons long ago left us and the one that was left adopted our sense of abandonment; Winter left without a goodbye, Spring never showed at all.

had we been better role models we would have been in a position to complain. instead, we walked the streets with long sleeves rolled and tried to smile:

– *How about this weather, huh?*

smiles.

4.2

high school's final years were spent in coffee shops.

giving all we had for a dwindling supply of burned beans further coloring tainted water. and what we had was not much: stained smiles that found a way to show themselves even when not earned. and there we were taught what institutions never could— atheism, satyriasis and cynicism. everyone had the same persecuted life. verbatim. but we learned to look at it in its proper context.

we traded away our first-round draft pick in the placement of our immortal soul for knowledgeable quips, curious women and another cup spiked with synthetic nicotine.

4.17

she tutored all the fledgling men.

no special qualifications save for a willingness and the immediate access to the tools of that specific tutoring trade. only a couple more years of experience but she had accessible rates and hours.

taking each into bedrooms with tinfoiled windows then— with taciturn enthusiasm —took out the same visuals each time: posterboard diagrams at half-scale and an eight-inch metallic pointer. mainly pointing at the same spot, stating and restating:

– *Never neglect here. See that there? Never neglect it.*
until each left feeling competent.

we heard her fall.

usually the most beautiful part— before gasps and tears, after the laughter and beating feet. someone as not-so-young as we were playfully forgetting that all joy had been forcibly removed until the ground tripped her. we turned toward the misplaced silence in time to see knees acknowledge this world as their master, leaking into sidewalk cracks before tears could do the same.

it was the creation of somedaysoon scars.

and— in thoughts of someday —we saw how beautiful she would eventually be when that late-teen stature gave way to a woman whose bedroom chronicles exchanged stories of scars with lovers. infallible proof of mortality. time together threatened by skin regrown in place with flaws: this is how life is emphasized.

we wanted to witness more of it.

we left iced coffee-like drinks to melt on sidewalk tables and drove around town trying to find more scarred silence. nothing seen in the passing hours giving out before motivation.

so we took to tripping strangers and breaking bottles on front stoops in front of taut triplines; we wristwatch reflected the sun into the eyes of inexperienced drivers; we weakened the legs of rusted trampolines; we rigged mailboxes to explode— we became junkies for the someday thankfulness they would all have for these actions.

she never shared a story of scars.

boyfriends were too interested in other parts.

she received those benign compliments all women grudgingly accept about eyes.

she had more than a dozen men mutter something— they perceived to be —complimentary about the dimples above her belt line in the back. most in bars but a few in the bedroom, too.

in truth, no one thought to look at her knees. legs? sure. but never knees.

and because no one said anything, she spent the first decade believing them to be aberrations— defects in beauty. then, when everything beautiful began to lose its shape and charm, she took to wearing short skirts and long socks; a dare for anyone to comment on marred flesh.

she was prepared.

she had a dozen stories at the ready— interesting lies to look interesting.

but no one ever asked.

5.13

high school doors were locked one day.

   diplomas distributed at random, each reading:

   – *Good luck.*

as we were forced into this combative world.

   out there were the ones waiting to die and the ones that wanted to watch all the others die first. there were siphoners of expensive fuel trying to keep inebriated cheaply. there were con men who spraypainted tangled coat hangers green and tumbled them loose in traffic to watch the collisions of people turning heads and steering wheels in belief they had seen one last living thing. there were forever deniers of December 33rd. there were oral sex virgins, women who were no one's first kiss and men who knew they wouldn't get more attractive with age. and, impossibly, there were fanatics.

   not churches. this slow decline revealed the long-preached cataclysmic apocalypse as an unwelcome lie; a thousand years of carefully marketed promotional material made defunct. grudgingly placating the dwindling attendance of the old with:

   – *Hell, go ahead and enjoy your lives now...*

that came too late.

   no, the fanatics were of the now— destined to die a bit faster than everyone else but enjoying it a bit more. nothing that the extremists of parents' time found fulfilling: ritual suicides, workplace shootings, sex and/or drugs. these— with the exception of drugs —were futile in a world of extinction; the exception only a way to forget.

   and they were not always too different from the rest until their excesses were stumbled upon: masturbating in public, fisticuffing someone who wanted nothing more than to live comfortably until the end, playing retro video games until an emaciated death. all done without regrets; resigned to the inevitability of pleasurable whims.

   we lived in a sheltered shadow of those fanatics up until

then— identical in actions save for the fact we had an irrational hope in change.

father fell farming the field.

no matter that the ground bore nothing— not even a blade of grass —for years; all had long ago dried to dust and abandoned the land, leaving father to lay there alone.

we knew it was inevitable.

father always said his heart was in the land— the only thing left out there to absorb the fertilizer and water while ignoring cursed pleas —and it failed; the last thing the land killed. impossible to prosecute or punish in any way save for carving a trench where he lay— which we did. all things become heavier in death, even if they do— simultaneously —become less burdensome. we planted father in the taciturn tormentor of shifting sand incapable of holding even one planted stone marker.

but the inevitable is still sometimes surprising. father left younger than most others in parents' generation who tried their hand at living, leaving friends and family with no proper eulogies prepared. so the large crowd gathered on standard fallbacks of:

– *A damn shame.*

– *Gone before his time...*

as well as the holdouts proclaiming:

– *God has His reasons...*

in a haughty and fearful tone, reasonably sure they were important enough to God to hold out many more years.

but all sidenote-added the only comforting cliché father would have agreed with:

– *He's in a better place now.*

a little more alone, we threw stones at stars.

skipping them among constellations, seeking a loose socket in those forever lights. but— when lucky enough to stumble one tumbling downward —they always fell out of reach— into the somewhere hands of someone lucky.

but that did not stop the stones from flying.

never done in the hope of holding the dwindling twinkle of a thousand wishes and an inevitably few sonnets.

we threw stones at stars to chase away nights outlasting their welcome— something that had to be done more often than not. darkness has a way of settling itself in the lonely places where things aren't thrown.

4.8

she lived where the stars fell.

a briefly illuminated ground every time the sky grew darker. an entire township spent sitting nights on porches— rifles at the ready to shoot each helpless star for another wish.

the first shootings brought botched wishes. everyone became rich without a thing in town to be purchased; strawberries and grandchildren decayed to dust before being enjoyed— wishes cannot defy the will of the world.

so before shooting stars, they collectively shout their more practical demands:

– One good night's sleep!

– Not to feel so hungry in this forever night!

– One dream— one REALISTIC dream —of the way it was!

one wish split a thousand ways so only a moment of satiation is given to each; a torment to be relived again and again as they continue to fall.

so we went east.

knowing if we did not abandon mother immediately then she would be reliant upon us to keep her indoors— resentful —cooking and expecting messes to be made.

and the path of father's childhood could not be mapped by stories— but we tried. oncewere borders didn't even have the remnants of signposts; we all inhabited the same state. and the ashes of buildings no longer held illustrated ceramic plates or key chains in the design of one destroyed monument or another. there probably wasn't a person living capable of finding these forgotten objects of awe— doubtful we would recognize them as such if they were stumbled upon.

the motels still remained— tucked off of highways — decrepit roofless buildings encircling a concrete divot in the land; open graves with no inhabitants.

we drove without sleep until the memories of father's stories ended— to where there should have been family. but we were incapable of identifying who should be notified of their blood ending in another.

but father's blood was never a known thing. so we simply shouted:

– *Another one is dead.*

and kept driving without looking to see if anyone took notice of the announcement.

she never appreciated subtle things.

every light touch down the spine needed to become a back rub.

every kiss goodbye was drawn out to make every first date a one-night-stand.

and smells— she never understood subtle smells. one stormy someday she opened every window in the house to catch the scent of lightning and rain without understanding that those overpowering things need to remain outside. every room became blended: the bedroom that smelled of two; shelved bathroom cleaning products permeating messes made; the kitchen scarred with oven-thawed foods forgotten; the mildewed mudroom; the dining room where wind-extinguished candles swirled and dissipated in the obviousness of what she had done— all carried away; replaced with unsubtle electricity and wind freeing themselves from closed windows; doors didn't stay locked forever and she was abandoned by both in differing directions.

leaving thunderstorms to carry in them the lost smells of what two people once were.

5.19

we were no longer given rainbows.

not something announced from a booming voice above. no. only when sitting with strangers in the remnants of a pub off of some holy highway in the newly unfamiliar smell of thunderstorms did someone innocuously ask:

– *When was the last time you saw a rainbow?*
and we all took to furrowing foreheads until a consensus was reached— not for near two decades. a forgotten promise. maybe simply broken or mistranslated or beyond the statute of limitations.

suddenly everyone watched the sky. boats were unburied from garages. federal departments were created to research the overlooked phenomena.

the skies had cleared when we saw some strange she brandishing a Punky Colour® dyed promise— from roots to bifurcated tips —in the letters of ROYGBIV that we would not be destroyed.

she turned to look at things not there.

each movement done to arc the hair in air.

familiar in the way some never-seen things can be.

but on the pillow the rainbow bent to reveal breaks between colors.

fingers combed thru the strands bled them into muddied gray deceptions as a new rain began to beat annunciations into the ceiling.

5.9

it was probably the last thing built.

some things were later modified. that guy in Alaska that made the news did not build one large ladder, simply duct taped old ladders together until he could see the stars from the point of view of other stars— telling tales of how Orion looks like a decomposed corpse from the vantage point of the first planet in the solar system circling the last light in Scorpio's tail. stars, like stories, become unintelligible when you too often alter their point of view.

we were never shown the uses for a level or taught the skills of channeling the assaulting sounds of a Skil saw into something constructive. so we amateurishly hammered thumbnails blackened until lost like the tips of some fingers sawed off that grew back all too slowly. but we built it: an unplumb bookshelf shrine in the car's backseat to travel as a display case of knowledge.

each new town had a library where we liberated something from their abandoned collection. shelves accumulated undulating rows of sideways texts reading like a documented sound wave; something from Edouard-Leon Scott de Martinville. proof of a knowledge acquired without an intention to be played back. a statement of:

  – *This is a unique collection of the uniqueness of others.*
as those leaning spines held the hopes of places and ideas that did not exist as we drove trying to find them. words were made— like women —for no other reason but to lie with— the only discovery left in a world strung thin with too much reality.

still, when the last nail found its place, that recurring voice began ringing in ears:

  – *This is not what you were meant to build.*

we set up a home somewhere where it snowed.

some one-room apartment surrounded by others in equally small spaces. everyone isolated among so many hidden by false niceties. there was not much within it: bookshelf brought in from the car and sheets strewn about in the corner because not even beds were made any longer. that was it.

living there for a thousand days before we were found by a woman who came around for a thousand nights— sometimes we would slip and call her by the name of the woman in the blue coat; she did not seem to mind... and it was only coincidence they shared the same name.

still, she did not show on night one thousand and one. and it did not take long for sheets to decay in her absence. no longer smelling of her on night one thousand and three; they simply smelled...

so we burned the apartment complex down by igniting sheets with drunkenly dropped faux-cigarettes— flaming isolated neighbors jumping from fatal heights, graves dug on contact in the white powder.

easier to destroy it all than to be reminded that something we once shared with such enthusiasm could go stale so quickly.

comforter corners were bungee wrapped to bed frames.

it was too much of a struggle on occasional mornings. a momentum of stagnation begins and a week or its ending would be lost between those covers like words in a book never read. pissing into the empty wine bottles toppled all around— long ago leaking the last of their crimson onto the floor; abortive reminders of stronger days.

she bungee-cord wrapped comforter corners to the bed frame for the struggle: the only way she felt something was accomplished by getting out of bed.

and— once out of bed —she was motivated to conquer other daily achievements. making the morning's first mixed drink strong so she felt the same when it was lifted.

5.19

eventually, most wore emotions on their sleeves.

seeing it again and again in each new town; yellow crayon-drawn faces on napkins or uncoiled toilet paper rolls or any other usable refuse— rubber band wrapped and displayed above the left bicep —emoting things sometimes forgotten how to emulate.

no more than six cards: a sedated grin; a large toothy smile; a redundantly blank stare; a frown; pouty lips accompanied by tears; a devilishly smirking face with horns.

that was it.

somehow enough to convey everything so many words were once needed to say.

4.18

she wore her devilishly smirking horned armband.

already knowing the way in— beyond outdated PRIVATE PROPERTY and NO TRESPASSING signs —thru a hole in the wooden fence. and she screamed sunken screams as beautiful hips built for no-longer things pried at surrounding boards that once allowed easy passage.

vintage bottles— housed in a box too big —had to be handed thru two-by-two as though entering the alcoholic's ark.

but she sat on the pitcher's mound with her man and a half-rack scattered around like a celebration— like something had been done that the few remaining stick and ball scholars would remember for eternity, even thru senility when the names of family members would be abandoned to keep space for those accolades.

so they sat on the pitcher's mound and among their slowly drained audience. when enough of them were gone, she threw them over home plate— or as close to home plate as she could get them. cheering with every KRACK as tho they were the crack of a bat and she was ignorant of the goal of the pitcher.

exhausted from imagined triumphs, the two of them lay on the pitcher's mound— clothes strewn beneath as haphazardly as bottles —and tried to do a devilish something worthy of remembrance—

she said:

– *You make my pelvis sob.*

while the adorned left arm pouted in mockery of a face forgetting how to do the same.

but she let eyes release real tears.

it took hours of observation spread over the course of a few evenings to confirm anything else could cry— but what she said was fact. tears leaked down her left leg in a marathon attempt to try and find someone worthy of spilling them.

she said:

– *It wouldn't be so bad if that was the only part you made cry...*

5.18

mother made a great mourner.

widowhood giving the definition motherhood never did. or— if it did the same defining —the former was preferred. each phoned homestead call gave mother a chance to relate a mood based on some post-mortem virtue falsely attributed to father. these sainthood recollections reshaped the story to be told into a silently industrious worker and a loving husband. that's it. no accounting for the fist-sized holes in walls or the fears and bruises of youth or the reason why mother never left the house— no explanation for unspoken tears the nights father never came home without accounting for nocturnal activities.

father's more indecorous deeds were retroactively stricken away from all recollections.

4.10

she shouted unreasonable commands during sex.

ready to flash the yellow card frown when each demand was done in an undesirable way. never elaborating more than one sentence statements:

– Uncompromise with the left side of your torso like a stroke victim.

– Hum a pop song with me in your mouth.

– Say, "I love you!"

– Sparkle.

thinking some joy could be found that way— coupling the absurd with a laborious act —but neither party ever did.

5.18

she rolled away.

waking with an almost-sense of accomplishing something— so often remaining in bed with the punishment of waking by herself. but she woke with company to prove some punishments are tolerable alternatives to misplaced rewards.

she blankly stared at the emotions strewn about the room the night before, wondering why they were all out of reach...

lying in bed with legs tangled like the torn sheets—

she shoulder-wore only a placid grin in post-orgasm quivers.

flesh folded upon itself indecipherably; not able to tell what was beard and what was bush, which holes belonged to whom and what to do to them. flesh folded upon itself and— before pulling apart —it was impossible to tell who was who.

and when bodies tried to break away, congealed fluids held tight; forced to sleep where they were— she rested her head in that divot where it is only natural for the butts of rifles and shotguns and the heads of women to rest.

in the morning her mouth went off like a shotgun blast in a silent overcast December day; but the way Decembers were thought of before they were everyday. earring left on the pillow while ears rang— shoulder throbbed —and she walked to the shower, naked, telling of nostalgic needs for no-longer-existent Chinese food.

eight months later:

mother said a bud of bone sprung from where a stone marker should have been. we tried to tell how the dirt devils and devil cones strip the dust away and soon all of father would be exposed in his new form. we thought to recommend a bible be placed on the land to deter such action but mother would not listen to the reasoning we all had outgrown.

mother said it was a skeletal plant growing from where we planted father.

not knowing what else to do, we told mother to water it— told where the last of the garage-stored petroleum-based nitrogen could be found. we infrequently called and mother told how it was growing into a petite ivory tree of red-veined green leaves. even that first seasonless season it— apparently —bore a flower of flesh on a bony limb barely capable of holding it; but it withered without bearing fruit.

all that was believable enough. sure, but mother pushed it too far, saying that the grass around it— actual grass —grew in radius. we joked it was because father was as unbearable to live with below ground as above and everything once planted was trying to escape; mother said it all simply needed something to lead by example.

we kept driving, tho. whichever way. never believing father gave life to the ground that took his.

4.11

she slept with drapes draped open.

a twin bed centered between so many picture windows— impossible to think of anything more than:

– *She is the person who should not throw stones.*

most single women sleep to the flickering blues of the television; near-mute voices rerunning tales of documented dead animals or the wars of dead men or preaching the ways we may live forever. or the radio; classical, talk, oldies. none mattering, only that a voice lets them know someone else is out there— becoming a habit forcing each to feel lonely without it.

even if someone else is sharing the bed.

but she left the drapes draped open; the antithesis of other single women.

such actions never go unnoticed; she gathered quite a following. the first few must have hidden— tucked in bushes or tree branches or idling cars. but it did not take long for men to know she needed an audience as rows of them sat in the sand that was once grass; no one ever doing anything— save for silently watching —as she undressed down to nothing but those white skivvies hugged tight to hips wanting to fall into the curves they constricted.

and as she slid legs under sheets— head upon pillow — and squirmed for comfort, the dozens of men simultaneously reclined themselves onto their sides— eyes still fixed on her. one of the last living women who did not feel lonely when others were around.

the land eventually ended.

nothing but water that fell off the horizon; hosting a rising sun instead of setting one but— even with that —it was nothing new. incessant water repeating itself. not knowing what else to do, we hopped an airplane to anywhere. eight, ten, twelve hours of flight in night. windows showed clouds as fixed as in mother's day, looking like little more than synthetic cotton glued to garbage bag blackness.

we landed while everyone aboard was asleep.

and— in the haze of waking —it all seemed new.

the distance displayed erect monuments and sidewalks were runways for strangers speaking nonsensical languages; we were held in hotel beds by a confused euphoria that first night. dreams of finding one place better found in daylight.

but the next day we recognized the same strangers saying the same nonsense and the tours of monuments were always at a distance, seen thru looking-glass amplification.

then it all crumbled— overstaying the mirage's longevity.

brushstrokes of backdrops showed. the extras stopped acting and spoke a lazy english instead of an accented one. even the motel beds became as familiarly uncomfortable as home— kindly offering up dreams of far-far-away because it knew we now knew we could never get there.

so we slept thru the flight back with plastic shutters pulled down; allowing illusionists to have their time to piece back together the land we never left.

4.4

we eventually returned home.

stopping in each bar on the long road there, recognizing faces but forgetting women we never should have. trying to compensate with generalities of:

– Hey... you! How've you been?
or the too-obvious:

– Hey... have you met my friend...?
then remained silent as they did the work; we probably forgot both names.

not that they were unmemorable.

it might have been we knew them too well— knew the way they breathed before sleep, the way that breathing slowed and steadied when sleep came; knew expressions they did not know they made; knew the song sung when thinking they were alone in a large house; knew their comfort foods and their phone number even tho it was phone-programmed ready to dial with one touch; knew all this and more... but not their names.

for some reason, it was one of the only things they expected to be remembered by...

when she finally met another she wanted to love?

she gave away every bit of her that could be called beautiful; and he took it. first it was expressions: a chin down, batted eye bit of coyness; wide eyes failing in attempted lies; a bitten lip of blood in ecstasy.

then it was movements: the sha-klack-clak heeled walk; contrapposto poses when caught in thought; a fingernail tapping of teeth when nervous.

then it was physical beauty: the vibrance of eyes; the richness of hair color; taut skin and youth.

then— finally —it was memories. all of the beautiful ones taken a night at a time until she woke one morning to scream at that unknown man found in bed.

still, she remembered a boy by a dying stream fondly— which, with nothing else left, finally became beautiful.

5.19

once home we witnessed the veracity of mother.

dressed in black, the hunched shadow of the remembered figure tending to the living tomb towering over the old estate. we watched from a distance— over the heads of hundreds of onlookers —and saw that the growing incantation of father was the first one mother loved since we were born— hers alone to tend for all the years we were away. still, this version was no less demanding; needing to be fed and groomed and cleaned up after after falling apart.

but they were silent demands.

these things matter and can set the tones for afterlives, too.

only after sundown— after the congregation had their fill of basking beneath the bone tree —did we catch mother's eye. even then, it was just a gesture to the fallen petals of flesh flowers from the tree. saying:

– Be a dear and rake those? I'll have dinner ready by the time it's done.

as tho we had never left.

and, as tho we had never left, we obeyed while cursing unheard— picking up each petal of father's complexion from the yard's green grass.

she came out of coincidence.

expecting to see nothing more than what the ground was giving again; the same pilgrimage so many of the so few still-living came to see.

the blue coat had seen better days.

so had she.

so had the man swinging from a bone branch pruning stray limbs, shouting the name she forgot to respond to—watching as he approached, taking an unoffered hand and waiting for the ending to begin.

we planned the wake the morning mother didn't.

only a few months after we returned, quietly tip-toeing thru the house out of habits learned those nights she held on to what father long ago lost and the ground long ago regained. we dialed the few acquaintances mother once possessed and invited the fewer not outlived.

they began arriving at seven. all looked into the exposed bedroom and saw mother with eyes closed in that tattered shirt always worn to bed; it set the mood— forcing them to whisper while drinks were somberly sipped from plastic cups, knowing mother would not be around to wash the glass ones.

no one was drunk enough to laugh loudly until ten. then it became contagious and everyone shared their best memories of the dead. we questioned their veracity with inquisitive eyes and confused smiles but no words; Death shapes the person no longer around contradicting desires to love them.

the jewelry box Etch-A-Sketch simply read:
– Do– not/bury– me/by– your– father—
and nothing more. no one knowing if that near-phobia was rooted in the ghastly branched memorial of bone or if the fear was nothing would happen in the shadow of father. or if it was because this world could never keep standing the things mother's father built.

whichever, the pyre was lit at midnight.

some drove themselves home afterward with near-sincere apologies. some curled on the grass and slept at the feet of the flames for warmth. the rest watched the smoke curl in mockery as it left us, carried by the breeze that carried mother's remains to the bone tree towering over the land— by dawn, the flesh flowers folded themselves closed.

She spread the blue coat beneath the tree.

At first, they sat there. The old times showed signs of leaving but it felt calamitous to speak of them until then—so they said nothing as she spread herself beneath the tree.

within a week the flowers bulged.

each looking like the stories told in remembrance of bellies riddled with life— this time there are hundreds on one bone frame.

we don't know what they will bring— if this is the love they had before the ground died or if it is something new— but we will soon be giving out like the ground long long ago did; left to hoping that the hundreds of fruits will let fall thousands of us in miniature.

or maybe the same thing was happening within the confines of the blue coat— building a new world instead of rebuilding the old.

whichever, someway we will be remembered.

4.20

About The Author

c.vance is the author of *the alley flowers bloom for every drunk who pisses on them save for me.* He co–hosts *Drunken Literates,* a podcast of irreverant discussions about books, followed by interviews with inebriated writers, publishers and other creative people. He works as a day laborer in Minneapolis, Minnesota.

About The Artist

Debra Di Dlasi (www.debradiblasi.com) is a multi-genre, multimedia writer and founding publisher of Jaded Ibis Productions and Jaded Ibis Press. She studied poetry with Larry Levis and Thomas McAfee before taking a degree in visual art from Kansas City Art Institute, where she also taught experimental writing forms between 1998-2003. Her art has been exhibited in museums and galleries in the U.S.